Parnassus On Wheels

Christopher Morley

Published: 1917
Categorie(s): Fiction, Humorous

About Morley:

Christopher Morley (5 May 1890 – 28 March 1957) was an American journalist, novelist, essayist and poet. He also produced stage productions for a few years and gave college lectures.

To H.B.F. and H.F.M.

A   LETTER   TO
David   Grayson,   Esq.
OF HEMPFIELD, U.S.A.

MY DEAR SIR,

Although my name appears on the title page, the real author of this book is Miss Helen McGill (now Mrs. Roger Mifflin), who told me the story with her own inimitable vivacity. And on her behalf I want to send to you these few words of acknowledgment.

Mrs. Mifflin, I need hardly say, is unskilled in the arts of authorship: this is her first book, and I doubt whether she will ever write another. She hardly realized, I think, how much her story owes to your own delightful writings. There used to be a well-thumbed copy of "Adventures in Contentment" on her table at the Sabine Farm, and I have seen her pick it up, after a long day in the kitchen, read it with chuckles, and say that the story of you and Harriet reminded her of herself and Andrew. She used to mutter something about "Adventures in Discontentment" and ask why Harriet's side of the matter was never told? And so when her own adventure came to pass, and she was urged to put it on paper, I think she unconsciously adopted something of the manner and matter that you have made properly yours.

Surely, sir, you will not disown so innocent a tribute! At any rate, Miss Harriet Grayson, whose excellent qualities we have all so long admired, will find in Mrs. Mifflin a kindred spirit.

Mrs. Mifflin would have said this for herself, with her characteristic definiteness of speech, had she not been out of touch with her publishers and foolscap paper. She and the Professor are on their Parnassus, somewhere on the high roads, happily engrossed in the most godly diversion known to man—selling books. And I venture to think that there are no volumes they take more pleasure in recommending than the wholesome and invigorating books which bear your name.

Believe me, dear Mr. Grayson, with warm regards,

Faithfully   yours,

CHRISTOPHER   MORLEY.

Chapter 1

I wonder if there isn't a lot of bunkum in higher education? I never found that people who were learned in logarithms and other kinds of poetry were any quicker in washing dishes or darning socks. I've done a good deal of reading when I could, and I don't want to "admit impediments" to the love of books, but I've also seen lots of good, practical folk spoiled by too much fine print. Reading sonnets always gives me hiccups, too.

I never expected to be an author! But I do think there are some amusing things about the story of Andrew and myself and how books broke up our placid life. When John Gutenberg, whose real name (so the Professor says) was John Gooseflesh, borrowed that money to set up his printing press he launched a lot of troubles on the world.

Andrew and I were wonderfully happy on the farm until he became an author. If I could have foreseen all the bother his writings were to cause us, I would certainly have burnt the first manuscript in the kitchen stove.

Andrew McGill, the author of those books every one reads, is my brother. In other words, I am his sister, ten years younger. Years ago Andrew was a business man, but his health failed and, like so many people in the story books, he fled to the country, or, as he called it, to the bosom of Nature. He and I were the only ones left in an unsuccessful family. I was slowly perishing as a conscientious governess in the brownstone region of New York. He rescued me from that and we bought a farm with our combined savings. We became real farmers, up with the sun and to bed with the same. Andrew wore overalls and a soft shirt and grew brown and tough. My hands got red and blue with soapsuds and frost; I never saw a Redfern advertisement from one year's end to another, and my kitchen was a battlefield where I set my teeth and learned to love hard work. Our literature was government agriculture reports, patent medicine almanacs, seedsmen's booklets, and Sears Roebuck catalogues. We subscribed to Farm and Fireside and read the serials aloud. Every now and then, for real excitement, we read something stirring in the Old Testament—that cheery book Jeremiah, for instance, of which Andrew was very fond. The farm did actually prosper, after a while; and Andrew used to hang over the pasture bars at sunset, and tell, from the way his pipe burned, just what the weather would be the next day.

As I have said, we were tremendously happy until Andrew got the fatal idea of telling the world how happy we were. I am sorry to have to admit he had always been rather a bookish man. In his college days he had edited the students' magazine, and sometimes he would get discontented with the Farm and Fireside serials and pull down his bound volumes of the college paper. He would read me some of his youthful poems and stories and mutter vaguely about writing something himself some day. I was more concerned with sitting hens than with sonnets and I'm bound to say I never took these threats very seriously. I should have been more severe.

Then great-uncle Philip died, and his carload of books came to us. He had been a college professor, and years ago when Andrew was a boy Uncle Philip had been very fond of him—had, in fact, put him through college. We were the only near relatives, and all those books turned up one fine day. That was the beginning of the end, if I had only known it. Andrew had the time of his life building shelves all round our living-room; not content with that he turned the old hen house into a study for himself, put in a stove, and used to sit up there evenings after I had gone to bed. The first thing I knew he called the place Sabine Farm (although it had been known for years as Bog Hollow) because he thought it a literary thing to do. He used to take a book along with him when he drove over to Redfield for supplies; sometimes the wagon would be two hours late coming home, with old Ben loafing along between the shafts and Andrew lost in his book.

I didn't think much of all this, but I'm an easy-going woman and as long as Andrew kept the farm going I had plenty to do on my own hook. Hot bread and coffee, eggs and preserves for breakfast; soup and hot meat, vegetables, dumplings, gravy, brown bread and white, huckleberry pudding, chocolate cake and buttermilk for dinner; muffins, tea, sausage rolls, blackberries and cream, and doughnuts for supper—that's the kind of menu I had been preparing three times a day for years. I hadn't any time to worry about what wasn't my business.

And then one morning I caught Andrew doing up a big, flat parcel for the postman. He looked so sheepish I just had to ask what it was.

"I've written a book," said Andrew, and he showed me the title page—

PARADISE REGAINED
BY
ANDREW McGILL

Even then I wasn't much worried, because of course I knew no one would print it. But Lord! a month or so later came a letter from a publisher—accepting it! That's the letter Andrew keeps framed above his desk. Just to show how such things sound I'll copy it here:

DECAMERON, JONES AND COMPANY
PUBLISHERS UNION SQUARE, NEW YORK

January 13, 1907.
DEAR MR. McGILL:
We have read with singular pleasure your manuscript "Paradise Regained." There is no doubt in our minds that so spirited an account of the joys of sane country living should meet with popular approval, and, with the exception of a few revisions and abbreviations, we would be glad to publish the book practically as it stands. We would like to have it illustrated by Mr. Tortoni, some of whose work you may have seen, and would be glad to know whether he may call upon you in order to acquaint himself with the local colour of your neighbourhood.
We would be glad to pay you a royalty of 10 percent upon the retail price of the book, and we enclose duplicate contracts for your signature in case this proves satisfactory to you.
Believe us, etc., etc.,
DECAMERON, JONES & CO.

I have since thought that "Paradise Lost" would have been a better title for that book. It was published in the autumn of 1907, and since that time our life has never been the same. By some mischance the book became the success of the season; it was widely commended as "a gospel of health and sanity" and Andrew received, in almost every mail, offers from publishers and magazine editors who wanted to get hold of his next book. It is almost incredible to what stratagems publishers will descend to influence an author. Andrew had written in "Paradise Regained" of the tramps who visit us, how quaint and appealing some of them are (let me add, how dirty), and how we never turn away any one who seems worthy. Would you believe that, in the spring after the book was published, a disreputable-looking vagabond with a knapsack, who turned up one day, blarneyed Andrew about his book and stayed overnight, announced himself at breakfast as a leading New York publisher? He had chosen this ruse in order to make Andrew's acquaintance.

You can imagine that it didn't take long for Andrew to become spoiled at this rate! The next year he suddenly disappeared, leaving only a note on the kitchen table, and tramped all over the state for six weeks collecting material for a new book. I had all I could do to keep him from going to New York to talk to editors and people of that sort. Envelopes of newspaper cuttings used to come to him, and he would pore over them when he ought to have been ploughing corn. Luckily the mail man comes along about the middle of the morning when Andrew is out in the fields, so I used to look over the letters before he saw them. After the second book ("Happiness and Hayseed" it was called) was printed, letters from publishers got so thick that I used to put them all in the stove before Andrew saw them—except those from the Decameron Jones people, which sometimes held checks. Literary folk used to turn up now and then to interview Andrew, but generally I managed to head them off.

But Andrew got to be less and less of a farmer and more and more of a literary man. He bought a typewriter. He would hang over the pigpen noting down adjectives for the sunset instead of mending the weather vane on the barn which took a slew so that the north wind came from the southwest. He hardly ever looked at the Sears Roebuck catalogues any more, and after Mr. Decameron came to visit us and suggested that Andrew write a book of country poems, the man became simply unbearable.

And all the time I was counting eggs and turning out three meals a day, and running the farm when Andrew got a literary fit and would go off on some vagabond jaunt to collect adventures for a new book. (I wish you could have seen the state he was in when he came back from these trips, hoboing it along the roads without any money or a clean sock to his back. One time he returned with a cough you could hear the other side of the barn, and I had to nurse him for three weeks.) When somebody wrote a little booklet about "The Sage of Redfield" and described me as a "rural Xantippe" and "the domestic balance-wheel that kept the great writer close to the homely realities of life" I made up my mind to give Andrew some of his own medicine. And that's my   story.

Chapter 2

It was a fine, crisp morning in fall—October I dare say—and I was in the kitchen coring apples for apple sauce. We were going to have roast pork for dinner with boiled potatoes and what Andrew calls Vandyke brown gravy. Andrew had driven over to town to get some flour and feed and wouldn't be back till noontime.

Being a Monday, Mrs. McNally, the washerwoman, had come over to take care of the washing. I remember I was just on my way out to the wood pile for a few sticks of birch when I heard wheels turn in at the gate. There was one of the fattest white horses I ever saw, and a queer wagon, shaped like a van. A funny-looking little man with a red beard leaned forward from the seat and said something. I didn't hear what it was, I was looking at that preposterous wagon of his.

It was coloured a pale, robin's-egg blue, and on the side, in big scarlet letters, was painted:

R. MIFFLIN'S TRAVELLING PARNASSUS GOOD BOOKS FOR SALE SHAKESPEARE, CHARLES LAMB, R.L.S. HAZLITT, AND ALL OTHERS

Underneath the wagon, in slings, hung what looked like a tent, together with a lantern, a bucket, and other small things. The van had a raised skylight on the roof, something like an old-fashioned trolley car; and from one corner went up a stove pipe. At the back was a door with little windows on each side and a flight of steps leading up to it.

As I stood looking at this queer turnout, the little reddish man climbed down from in front and stood watching me. His face was a comic mixture of pleasant drollery and a sort of weather-beaten cynicism. He had a neat little russet beard and a shabby Norfolk jacket. His head was very bald.

"Is this where Andrew McGill lives?" he said.

I admitted it.

"But he's away until noon," I added. "He'll be back then. There's roast pork for dinner."

"And apple sauce?" said the little man.

"Apple sauce and brown gravy," I said. "That's why I'm sure he'll be home on time. Sometimes he's late when there's boiled dinner, but never on roast pork days. Andrew would never do for a rabbi."

A sudden suspicion struck me.

"You're not another publisher, are you?" I cried. "What do you want with Andrew?"

"I was wondering whether he wouldn't buy this outfit," said the little man, including, with a wave of the hand, both van and white horse. As he spoke he released a hook somewhere, and raised the whole side of his wagon like a flap. Some kind of catch clicked, the flap remained up like a roof, displaying nothing but books— rows and rows of them. The flank of his van was nothing but a big bookcase. Shelves stood above shelves, all of them full of books—both old and new. As I stood gazing, he pulled out a printed card from somewhere and gave it to me:

ROGER MIFFLIN'S TRAVELLING PARNASSUS

Worthy friends, my wain doth hold
Many a book, both new and old;
Books, the truest friends of man,
Fill this rolling caravan.
Books to satisfy all uses,
Golden lyrics of the Muses,
Books on cookery and farming,
Novels passionate and charming,
Every kind for every need
So that he who buys may read.
What librarian can surpass us?

MIFFLIN'S TRAVELLING PARNASSUS

By R. Mifflin, Prop'r.
Star Job Print, Celeryville, Va.

While I was chuckling over this, he had raised a similar flap on the other side of the Parnassus which revealed still more shelves loaded with books.

I'm afraid I am severely practical by nature.

"Well!" I said, "I should think you *would* need a pretty stout steed to lug that load along. It must weigh more than a coal wagon."

"Oh, Peg can manage it all right," he said. "We don't travel very fast. But look here, I want to sell out. Do you suppose your husband would buy the outfit—Parnassus, Pegasus, and all? He's fond of books, isn't he?

"Hold on a minute!" I said. "Andrew's my brother, not my husband, and he's altogether *too* fond of books. Books'll be the ruin of this farm pretty soon. He's mooning about over his books like a sitting hen about half the time, when he ought to be mending harness. Lord, if he saw this wagonload of yours he'd be unsettled for a week. I have to stop the postman down the road and take all the publishers' catalogues out of the

14

mail so that Andrew don't see 'em. I'm mighty glad he's not here just now, I can tell you!"

I'm not literary, as I said before, but I'm human enough to like a good book, and my eye was running along those shelves of his as I spoke. He certainly had a pretty miscellaneous collection. I noticed poetry, essays, novels, cook books, juveniles, school books, Bibles, and what not—all jumbled together.

"Well, see here," said the little man—and about this time I noticed that he had the bright eyes of a fanatic— "I've been cruising with this Parnassus going on seven years. I've covered the territory from Florida to Maine and I reckon I've injected about as much good literature into the countryside as ever old Doc Eliot did with his five-foot shelf. I want to sell out now. I'm going to write a book about 'Literature Among the Farmers,' and want to settle down with my brother in Brooklyn and write it. I've got a sackful of notes for it. I guess I'll just stick around until Mr. McGill gets home and see if he won't buy me out. I'll sell the whole concern, horse, wagon, and books, for $400. I've read Andrew McGill's stuff and I reckon the proposition'll interest him. I've had more fun with this Parnassus than a barrel of monkeys. I used to be a school teacher till my health broke down. Then I took this up and I've made more than expenses and had the time of my life."

"Well, Mr. Mifflin," I said, "if you want to stay around I guess I can't stop you. But I'm sorry you and your old Parnassus ever came this way."

I turned on my heel and went back to the kitchen. I knew pretty well that Andrew would go up in the air when he saw that wagonload of books and one of those crazy cards with Mr. Mifflin's poetry on it.

I must confess that I was considerably upset. Andrew is just as unpractical and fanciful as a young girl, and always dreaming of new adventures and rambles around the country. If he ever saw that travelling Parnassus he'd fall for it like snap. And I knew Mr. Decameron was after him for a new book anyway. (I'd intercepted one of his letters suggesting another "Happiness and Hayseed" trip just a few weeks before. Andrew was away when the letter came. I had a suspicion what was in it; so I opened it, read it, and—well, burnt it. Heavens! as though Andrew didn't have enough to do without mooning down the road like a tinker, just to write a book about it.)

As I worked around the kitchen I could see Mr. Mifflin making himself at home. He unhitched his horse, tied her up to the fence, sat down by the wood pile, and lit a pipe. I could see I was in for it. By and by I couldn't stand it any longer. I went out to talk to that bald-headed pedlar.

"See here," I said. "You're a pretty cool fish to make yourself so easy in my yard. I tell you I don't want you around here, you and your travelling parcheesi. Suppose you clear out of here before my brother gets back and don't be breaking up our happy family."

"Miss McGill," he said (the man had a pleasant way with him, too—darn him—with his bright, twinkling eye and his silly little beard), "I'm sure I don't want to be discourteous. If you move me on from here, of course I'll go; but I warn you I shall lie in wait for Mr. McGill just down this road. I'm here to sell this caravan of culture, and by the bones of Swinburne I think your brother's the man to buy it."

My blood was up now, and I'll admit that I said my next without proper calculation.

"Rather than have Andrew buy your old parcheesi," I said, "I'll buy it myself. I'll give you $300 for it."

The little man's face brightened. He didn't either accept or decline my offer. (I was frightened to death that he'd take me right on the nail and bang would go my three years' savings for a Ford.)

"Come and have another look at her," he said.

I must admit that Mr. Roger Mifflin had fixed up his van mighty comfortably inside. The body of the wagon was built out on each side over the wheels, which gave it an unwieldy appearance but made extra room for the bookshelves. This left an inside space about five feet wide and nine long. On one side he had a little oil stove, a flap table, and a cozy-looking bunk above which was built a kind of chest of drawers—to hold clothes and such things, I suppose; on the other side more bookshelves, a small table, and a little wicker easy chair. Every possible inch of space seemed to be made useful in some way, for a shelf or a hook or a hanging cupboard or something. Above the stove was a neat little row of pots and dishes and cooking usefuls. The raised skylight made it just possible to stand upright in the centre aisle of the van; and a little sliding window opened onto the driver's seat in front. Altogether it was a very neat affair. The windows in front and back were curtained and a pot of geraniums stood on a diminutive shelf. I was amused to see a sandy Irish terrier curled up on a bright Mexican blanket in the bunk.

"Miss McGill," he said, "I couldn't sell Parnassus for less than four hundred. I've put twice that much into her, one time and another. She's built clean and solid all through, and there's everything a man would need from blankets to bouillon cubes. The whole thing's yours for $400—including dog, cook stove, and everything—jib, boom, and spanker. There's a tent in a sling underneath, and an ice box (he pulled up a little trap door under the bunk) and a tank of coal oil and Lord knows what all. She's as good as a yacht; but I'm tired of her. If you're so afraid of your brother taking a fancy to her, why don't you buy her yourself and go off on a lark?

Make *him* stay home and mind the farm!... Tell you what I'll do. I'll start you on the road myself, come with you the first day and show you how it's worked. You could have the time of your life in this thing, and give yourself a fine vacation. It would give your brother a good surprise, too. Why not?"

I don't know whether it was the neatness of his absurd little van, or the madness of the whole proposition, or just the desire to have an adventure of my own and play a trick on Andrew, but anyway, some extraordinary impulse seized me and I roared with laughter.

"Right!" I said. "I'll do it."

I, Helen McGill, in the thirty-ninth year of my age!

Chapter 3

"Well," I thought, "if I'm in for an adventure I may as well be spry about it. Andrew'll be home by half-past twelve and if I'm going to give him the slip I'd better get a start. I suppose he'll think I'm crazy! He'll follow me, I guess. Well, he just shan't catch me, that's all!" A kind of anger came over me to think that I'd been living on that farm for nearly fifteen years—yes, sir, ever since I was twenty-five—and hardly ever been away except for that trip to Boston once a year to go shopping with cousin Edie. I'm a home-keeping soul, I guess, and I love my kitchen and my preserve cupboard and my linen closet as well as grandmother ever did, but something in that blue October air and that crazy little red-bearded man just tickled me.

"Look here, Mr. Parnassus," I said, "I guess I'm a fat old fool but I just believe I'll do that. You hitch up your horse and van and I'll go pack some clothes and write you a check. It'll do Andrew all the good in the world to have me skip. I'll get a chance to read a few books, too. It'll be as good as going to college!" And I untied my apron and ran for the house. The little man stood leaning against a corner of the van as if he were stupefied. I dare say he was.

I ran into the house through the front door, and it struck me as comical to see a copy of one of Andrew's magazines lying on the living-room table with "The Revolt of Womanhood" printed across it in red letters. "Here goes for the revolt of Helen McGill," I thought. I sat down at Andrew's desk, pushed aside a pad of notes he had been jotting down about "the magic of autumn," and scrawled a few lines:

DEAR ANDREW,

Don't be thinking I'm crazy. I've gone off for an adventure. It just came over me that you've had all the adventures while I've been at home baking bread. Mrs. McNally will look after your meals and one of her girls can come over to do the housework. So don't worry. I'm going off for a little while—a month, maybe—to see some of this happiness and hayseed of yours. It's what the magazines call the revolt of womanhood. Warm underwear in the cedar chest in the spare room when you need it. With love, HELEN.

I left the note on his desk.

Mrs. McNally was bending over the tubs in the laundry. I could see only the broad arch of her back and hear the vigorous zzzzzzz of her rubbing. She straightened up at my call.

"Mrs. McNally," I said, "I'm going away for a little trip. You'd better let the washing go until this afternoon and get Andrew's dinner for him. He'll be back about twelve-thirty. It's half-past ten now. You tell him I've gone over to see Mrs. Collins at Locust Farm."

Mrs. McNally is a brawny, slow-witted Swede. "All right Mis' McGill," she said. "You be back to denner?"

"No, I'm not coming back for a month," I said. "I'm going away for a trip. I want you to send Rosie over here every day to do the housework while I'm away.

You can arrange with Mr. McGill about that. I've got to hurry now."

Mrs. McNally's honest eyes, as blue as Copenhagen china, gazing through the window in perplexity, fell upon the travelling Parnassus and Mr. Mifflin backing Pegasus into the shafts. I saw her make a valiant effort to comprehend the sign painted on the side of the van— and give it up.

"You going driving?" she said blankly.

"Yes," I said, and fled upstairs.

I always keep my bank book in an old Huyler box in the top drawer of my bureau. I don't save very quickly, I'm afraid. I have a little income from some money father left me, but Andrew takes care of that. Andrew pays all the farm expenses, but the housekeeping accounts fall to me. I make a fairish amount of pin money on my poultry and some of my preserves that I send to Boston, and on some recipes of mine that I send to a woman's magazine now and then; but generally my savings don't amount to much over $10 a month. In the last five years I had put by something more than $600. I had been saving up for a Ford. But just now it looked to me as if that Parnassus would be more fun than a Ford ever could be. Four hundred dollars was a lot of money, but I thought of what it would mean to have Andrew come home and buy it. Why, he'd be away until Thanksgiving! Whereas if I bought it I could take it away, have my adventure, and sell it somewhere so that Andrew never need see it. I hardened my heart and determined to give the Sage of Redfield some of his own medicine.

My balance at the Redfield National Bank was $615.20. I sat down at the table in my bedroom where I keep my accounts and wrote out a check to Roger Mifflin for $400. I put in plenty of curlicues after the figures so that no one could raise the check into

21

$400,000; then I got out my old rattan suit case and put in some clothes. The whole business didn't take me ten minutes. I came downstairs to find Mrs. McNally looking sourly at the Parnassus from the kitchen door.

"You going away in that—that 'bus, Mis' McGill?" she asked.

"Yes, Mrs. McNally," I said cheerfully. Her use of the word gave me an inspiration. "That's one of the new jitney 'buses we hear about. He's going to take me to the station. Don't you worry about me. I'm going for a holiday. You get Mr. McGill's dinner ready for him. After dinner tell him there's a note for him in the living-room."

"I tank that bane a queer 'bus," said Mrs. McNally, puzzled. I think the excellent woman suspected an elopement.

I carried my suit case out to the Parnassus. Pegasus stood placidly between the shafts. From within came sounds of vigorous movement. In a moment the little man burst out with a bulging portmanteau in his hand. He had a tweed cap slanted on the back of his head.

"There!" he cried triumphantly. "I've packed all my personal effects clothes and so on—and everything else goes with the transaction. When I get on the train with this bag I'm a free man, and hurrah for Brooklyn! Lord, won't I be glad to get back to the city! I lived in Brooklyn once, and I haven't been back there for ten years," he added plaintively.

"Here's the check," I said, handing it to him. He flushed a little, and looked at me rather shamefacedly. "See here," he said, "I hope you're not making a bad bargain? I don't want to take advantage of a lady. If you think your brother...."

"I was going to buy a Ford, anyway," I said, "and it looks to me as though this parcheesi of yours would be cheaper to run than any flivver that ever came out of

Detroit. I want to keep it away from Andrew and that's the main thing. You give me a receipt and we'll get away from here before he comes back."

He took the check without a word, hoisted his fat portmanteau on the driver's seat, and then disappeared in the van. In a minute he reappeared. On the back of one of his poetical cards he had written:

> Received from Miss McGill the sum of four
> hundred dollars in exchange for one
> Travelling Parnassus in first class condition,
> delivered to her this day, October 3rd, 19—.
> Signed
> ROGER MIFFLIN.

"Tell me," I said, "does your Parnassus— *my* Parnassus, rather—contain everything I'm likely to need? Is it stocked up with food and so on?"

"I was coming to that," he said. "You'll find a fair supply of stuff in the cupboard over the stove, though I used to get most of my meals at farmhouses along the road. I generally read aloud to people as I go along, and they're often good for a free meal. It's amazing how little most of the country folk know about books, and how pleased they are to hear good stuff. Down in Lancaster County, Pennsylvania...."

"Well, how about the horse?" I said hastily, seeing him about to embark on an anecdote. It wasn't far short of eleven o'clock, and I was anxious to get started.

"It might be well to take along some oats. My supply's about exhausted."

I filled a sack with oats in the stable and Mr. Mifflin showed me where to hang it under the van. Then in the kitchen I loaded a big basket with provisions for an emergency: a dozen eggs, a jar of sliced bacon, butter, cheese, condensed milk, tea, biscuits, jam, and two

23

loaves of bread. These Mr. Mifflin stowed inside the van, Mrs. McNally watching in amazement.

"I tank this bane a queer picnic!" she said. "Which way are you going? Mr. McGill, is he coming after you?"

"No," I insisted, "he's not coming. I'm going off on a holiday. You get dinner for him and he won't worry about anything until after that. Tell him I've gone over to see Mrs. Collins."

I climbed the little steps and entered my Parnassus with a pleasant thrill of ownership. The terrier on the bunk jumped to the floor with a friendly wag of the tail. I piled the bunk with bedding and blankets of my own, shook out the drawers which fitted above the bunk, and put into them what few belongings I was taking with me. And we were ready to start.

Redbeard was already sitting in front with the reins in hand. I climbed up beside him. The front seat was broad but uncushioned, well sheltered by the peak of the van. I gave a quick glance around at the comfortable house under its elms and maples—saw the big, red barn shining in the sun and the pump under the grape arbour. I waved good-bye to Mrs. McNally who was watching us in silent amazement. Pegasus threw her solid weight against the traces and Parnassus swung round and rolled past the gate. We turned into the Redfield road.

"Here," said Mifflin, handing me the reins, "you're skipper, you'd better drive. Which way do you want to go?"

My breath came a little fast when I realized that my adventure   had   begun!

Chapter 4

Just out of sight of the farm the road forks, one way running on to Walton where you cross the river by a covered bridge, the other swinging down toward Greenbriar and Port Vigor. Mrs. Collins lives a mile or so up the Walton road, and as I very often run over to see her I thought Andrew would be most likely to look for me there. So, after we had passed through the grove, I took the right-hand turn to Greenbriar. We began the long ascent over Huckleberry Hill and as I smelt the fresh autumn odour of the leaves I chuckled a little.

Mr. Mifflin seemed in a perfect ecstasy of high spirits. "This is certainly grand," he said. "Lord, I applaud your spunk. Do you think Mr. McGill will give chase?"

"I haven't an idea," I said. "Not right away, anyhow. He's so used to my settled ways that I don't think he'll suspect anything till he finds my note. I wonder what kind of story Mrs. McNally will tell!"

"How about putting him off the scent?" he said. "Give me your handkerchief."

I did so. He hopped nimbly out, ran back down the hill (he was a spry little person in spite of his bald crown), and dropped the handkerchief on the Walton Road about a hundred feet beyond the fork. Then he followed me up the slope.

"There," he said, grinning like a kid, "that'll fool him. The Sage of Redfield will undoubtedly follow a false spoor and the criminals will win a good start. But I'm afraid it's rather easy to follow a craft as unusual as Parnassus."

"Tell me how you manage the thing," I said. "Do you really make it pay?" We halted at the top of the hill to give Pegasus a breathing space. The terrier lay down in the dust and watched us gravely. Mr. Mifflin pulled out a pipe and begged my permission to smoke.

"It's rather comical how I first got into it," he said. "I was a school teacher down in Maryland. I'd been plugging away in a country school for years, on a starvation salary. I was trying to support an invalid mother, and put by something in case of storms. I remember how I used to wonder whether I'd ever be able to wear a suit that wasn't shabby and have my shoes polished every day. Then my health went back on me. The doctor told me to get into the open air. By and by I got this idea of a travelling bookstore. I had always been a lover of books, and in the days when I boarded out among the farmers I used to read aloud to them. After my mother died I built the wagon to suit my own ideas, bought a stock of books from a big second-hand store in Baltimore, and set out. Parnassus just about saved my life I guess."

He pushed his faded old cap back on his head and relit his pipe. I clicked to Pegasus and we rumbled gently off over the upland, looking down across the pastures. Distant cow bells sounded tankle-tonk among the bushes. Across the slope of the hill I could see the road winding away to Redfield. Somewhere along that road Andrew would be rolling back toward home and roast pork with apple sauce; and here was I, setting out on the first madness of my life without even a qualm.

"Miss McGill," said the little man, "this rolling pavilion has been wife, doctor, and religion to me for seven years. A month ago I would have scoffed at the thought of leaving her; but somehow it's come over me I need a change. There's a book I've been yearning to write for a long time, and I need a desk steady under my elbows and a roof over my head. And silly as it seems, I'm crazy to get back to Brooklyn. My brother and I used to live there as kids. Think of walking over the old Bridge at sunset and seeing the towers of Manhattan against a red sky! And those old gray cruisers down in the Navy Yard! You don't know how tickled I am to sell out. I've sold a lot of copies of your brother's books and I've often thought he'd be the man to buy Parnassus if I got tired of her."

"So he would," I said. "Just the man. He'd be only too likely to—and go maundering about in this jaunting car and neglect the farm. But tell me about selling books. How much profit do you make out of it? We'll be passing Mrs. Mason's farm, by and by, and we might as well sell her something just to make a start."

"It's very simple," he said. "I replenish my stock whenever I go through a big town. There's always a second-hand bookstore somewhere about, where you can pick up odds and ends. And every now and then I write to a wholesaler in New York for some stuff. When I buy a book I mark in the back just what I paid for it, then I know what I can afford to sell it for. See here."

He pulled up a book from behind the seat—a copy of "Lorna Doone" it was—and showed me the letters *a m* scrawled in pencil in the back.

"That means that I paid ten cents for this. Now, if you sell it for a quarter you've got a safe profit. It costs me about four dollars a week to run Parnassus—generally less. If you clear that much in six days you can afford to lay off on Sundays!"

"How do you know that *a m* stands for ten cents?" I asked.

"The code word's *manuscript*. Each letter stands for a figure, from 0 up to 9, see?" He scrawled it down on a scrap of paper:

m a n u s c r i p t 0 1 2 3 4 5 6 7 8 9

"Now, you see *a m* stands for 10, *a n* would be 12, *n s* is 24, *a c* is 15, *a m m* is $1.00, and so on. I don't pay much over fifty cents for books as a rule, because country folks are shy of paying much for them. They'll pay a lot for a separator or a buggy top, but they've never been taught to worry about literature! But it's surprising how excited they get about books if you sell 'em the right kind. Over beyond Port Vigor there's a farmer who's waiting for me to go back—I've been there three or four times—and he'll buy about five dollars' worth if I know him. First time I went there I sold him 'Treasure Island,' and he's talking about it yet. I sold him 'Robinson Crusoe,' and 'Little Women' for his daughter, and 'Huck Finn,' and Grubb's book about 'The Potato.' Last time I was there he wanted some Shakespeare, but I wouldn't give it to him. I didn't think he was up to it yet."

I began to see something of the little man's idealism in his work. He was a kind of traveling missionary in his way. A hefty talker, too. His eyes were twinkling now and I could see him warming up.

"Lord!" he said, "when you sell a man a book you don't sell him just twelve ounces of paper and ink and glue—you sell him a whole new life. Love and friendship and humour and ships at sea by night— there's all heaven and earth in a book, a real book I mean. Jiminy! If I were the baker or the butcher or the broom huckster, people would run to the gate when I came by—just waiting for my stuff. And here I go loaded with everlasting salvation—yes, ma'am, salvation for their little, stunted minds—and it's hard to make 'em see it. That's what makes it worth while—I'm doing something that nobody else from Nazareth, Maine, to Walla Walla, Washington, has ever thought of. It's a new field, but by the bones of Whitman it's worth while. That's what this country needs—more books!"

He laughed at his own vehemence. "Do you know, it's comical," he said. "Even the publishers, the fellows that print the books, can't see what I'm doing for them. Some of 'em refuse me credit because I sell their books for what they're worth instead of for the prices they mark on them. They write me letters about price-maintenance—and I write back about merit-maintenance. Publish a good book and I'll get a good price for it, Say I! Sometimes I think the publishers know less about books than any one else! I guess that's natural, though. Most school teachers don't know much about children."

"The best of it is," he went on, "I have such a darn good time. Peg and Bock (that's the dog) and I go loafing along the road on a warm summer day, and by and by we'll fetch up alongside some boarding-house and there are the boarders all rocking off their lunch on the veranda. Most of 'em bored to death—nothing good to read, nothing to do but sit and watch the flies buzzing in the sun and the chickens rubbing up and down in the dust. First thing you know I'll sell half a dozen books that put the love of life into them, and they don't forget Parnassus in a hurry. Take O. Henry, for instance—there isn't anybody so dog-gone sleepy that he won't enjoy that man's stories. He understood life, you bet, and he could write it down with all its little twists. I've spent an evening reading O. Henry and Wilkie Collins to people and had them buy out all their books I had and clamour for more."

"What do you do in winter?" I asked—a practical question, as most of mine are.

"That depends on where I am when bad weather sets in," said Mr. Mifflin. "Two winters I was down south and managed to keep Parnassus going all through the season. Otherwise, I just lay up wherever I am. I've never found it hard to get lodging for Peg and a job for myself, if I had to have them. Last winter I worked in a bookstore in Boston. Winter before, I was in a country drugstore down in Pennsylvania. Winter before that, I tutored a couple of small boys in English literature. Winter before that, I was a steward on a steamer; you see how it goes. I've had a fairly miscellaneous experience. As far as I can see, a man who's fond of books never need starve! But this winter I'm planing to live with my brother in Brooklyn and slog away at my book. Lord, how I've pondered over that thing! Long summer afternoons I've sat here, jogging along in the dust, thinking it out until it seemed as if my forehead would burst. You see, my idea is that the common people—in the country, that is—never have had any chance to get hold of books, and never have had any one to explain what books can mean. It's all right for college presidents to draw up their five-foot shelves of great literature, and for the publishers to advertise sets of their Linoleum Classics, but what the people need is the good, homely, honest stuff—something that'll stick to their ribs—make them laugh and tremble and feel sick to think of the littleness of this popcorn ball spinning in space without ever even getting a hot-box! And something that'll spur 'em on to keep the hearth well swept and the wood pile split into kindling and the dishes washed and dried and put away. Any one who can get the country people to read something worth while is doing his nation a real service. And that's what this caravan of culture aspires to.... You must be weary of this harangue! Does the Sage of Redfield ever run on like that?"

"Not to me," I said. "He's known me so long that he thinks of me as a kind of animated bread-baking and cake-mixing machine. I guess he doesn't put much stock in my judgment in literary matters. But he puts his digestion in my hands without reserve. There's Mason's farm over there. I guess we'd better sell them some books—hadn't we? Just for a starter."

We turned into the lane that runs up to the Mason farmhouse. Bock trotted on ahead—very stiff on his legs and his tail gently wagging—to interview the mastiff, and Mrs. Mason who was sitting on the porch, peeling potatoes, laid down the pan. She's a big, buxom woman with jolly, brown eyes like a cow's.

"For heaven's sake, Miss McGill," she called out in a cheerful voice—"I'm glad to see you. Got a lift, did you?"

She hadn't really noticed the inscription on Parnassus, and thought it was a regular huckster's wagon.

"Well, Mrs. Mason," I said, "I've gone into the book business. This is Mr. Mifflin. I've bought out his stock. We've come to sell you some books."

She laughed. "Go on, Helen," she said, "you can't kid me! I bought a whole set of books last year from an agent—'The World's Great Funeral Orations'—twenty volumes. Sam and I ain't read more'n the first volume yet. It's awful uneasy reading!"

Mifflin jumped down, and raised the side flap of the wagon. Mrs. Mason came closer. I was tickled to see how the little man perked up at the sight of a customer. Evidently selling books was meat and drink to him.

"Madam," he said, "'Funeral Orations' (bound in sackcloth, I suppose?) have their place, but Miss McGill and I have got some real books here to which I invite your attention. Winter will be here soon, and you will

31

need something more cheerful to beguile your evenings. Very possibly you have growing children who would profit by a good book or two. A book of fairy tales for the little girl I see on the porch? Or stories of inventors for that boy who is about to break his neck jumping from the barn loft? Or a book about road making for your husband? Surely there is something here you need? Miss McGill probably knows your tastes."

That little red-bearded man was surely a born salesman. How he guessed that Mr. Mason was the road commissioner in our township, goodness only knows. Perhaps it was just a lucky shot. By this time most of the family had gathered around the van, and I saw Mr. Mason coming from the barn with his twelve-year-old Billy.

"Sam," shouted Mrs. Mason, "here's Miss McGill turned book pedlar and got a preacher with her!"

"Hello, Miss McGill," said Mr. Mason. He is a big, slow-moving man of great gravity and solidity. "Where's Andrew?"

"Andrew's coming home for roast pork and apple sauce," I said, "and I'm going off to sell books for a living. Mr. Mifflin here is teaching me how. We've got a book on road mending that's just what you need."

I saw Mr. and Mrs. Mason exchange glances. Evidently they thought me crazy. I began to wonder whether we had made a mistake in calling on people I knew so well. The situation was a trifle embarrassing.

Mr. Mifflin came to the rescue.

"Don't be alarmed, sir," he said to Mr. Mason. "I haven't kidnapped Miss McGill." (As he is about half my size this was amusing.) "We are trying to increase her brother's income by selling his books for him. As a matter of fact, we have a wager with him that we can sell fifty copies of 'Happiness and Hayseed' before Hallowe'en. Now I'm sure your sporting instinct will assist us by taking at least one copy. Andrew McGill is probably the greatest author in this State, and every taxpayer ought to possess his books. May I show you a copy?"

"That sounds reasonable," said Mr. Mason, and he almost smiled. "What do you say, Emma, think we better buy a book or two? You know those 'Funeral Orations.'..." "Well," said Emma, "you know we've always said we ought to read one of Andrew McGill's books but we didn't rightly know how to get hold of one. That fellow that sold us the funeral speeches didn't seem to know about 'em. I tell you what, you folks better stop and have dinner with us and you can tell us what we'd ought to buy. I'm just ready to put the potatoes on the stove now."

I must confess that the prospect of sitting down to a meal I hadn't cooked myself appealed to me strongly; and I was keen to see what kind of grub Mrs. Mason provided for her house-hold; but I was afraid that if we dallied there too long Andrew would be after us. I was about to say that we would have to be getting on, and couldn't stay; but apparently the zest of expounding his philosophy to new listeners was too much for Mifflin. I heard him saying:

"That's mighty kind of you, Mrs. Mason, and we'd like very much to stay. Perhaps I can put Peg up in your barn for a while. Then we can tell you all about our books." And to my amazement I found myself chiming in with assent.

Mifflin certainly surpassed himself at dinner. The fact that Mrs. Mason's hot biscuits tasted of saleratus gave me far less satisfaction than it otherwise would, because I was absorbed in listening to the little vagabond's talk. Mr. Mason came to the table grumbling something about his telephone being out of order—(I wondered whether he had been trying to get Andrew on the wire;

he was a little afraid that I was being run away with, I think)—but he was soon won over by the current of the little man's cheery wit. Nothing daunted Mifflin. He talked to the old grandmother about quilts; offered to cut off a strip of his necktie for her new patchwork; and told all about the illustrated book on quilts that he had in the van. He discussed cookery and the Bible with Mrs. Mason; and she being a leading light in the Greenbriar Sunday School, was pleasantly scandalized by his account of the best detective stories in the Old Testament. With Mr. Mason he was all scientific farming, chemical manures, macadam roads, and crop rotation; and to little Billy (who sat next him) he told extraordinary yarns about Daniel Boone, Davy Crockett, Kit Carson, Buffalo Bill, and what not. Honestly I was amazed at the little man. He was as genial as a cricket on the hearth, and yet every now and then his earnestness would break through. I don't wonder he was a success at selling books. That man could sell clothes pins or Paris garters, I guess, and make them seem romantic.

"You know, Mr. Mason," he said, "you certainly owe it to these youngsters of yours to put a few really good books into their hands. City kids have the libraries to go to, but in the country there's only old Doc Hostetter's Almanac and the letters written by ladies with backache telling how Peruna did for them. Give this boy and girl of yours a few good books and you're starting them on the double-track, block-signal line to happiness. Now there's 'Little Women'—that girl of yours can learn more about real girlhood and fine womanhood out of that book than from a year's paper dolls in the attic."

"That's right, Pa," assented Mrs. Mason. ("Go on with your meal, Professor, the meat'll be cold.") She was completely won by the travelling bookseller, and had given him the highest title of honour in her ken. "Why, I read that story when I was a girl, and I still remember it. That's better readin' for Dorothy than those funeral speeches, I reckon. I believe the Professor's right: we'd ought to have more books laying around. Seems kind of a shame, with a famous author at the next farm, not to read more, don't it, now?"

So by the time we got down to Mrs. Mason's squash pie (good pie, too, I admit, but her hand is a little heavy for pastry), the whole household was enthusiastic about books, and the atmosphere was literary enough for even Dr. Eliot to live in without panting. Mrs. Mason opened up her parlour and we sat there while Mifflin recited "The Revenge" and "Maud Muller."

"Well, now, ain't that real sweet!" said Emma Mason. "It's surprising how those words rhyme so nicely. Seems almost as though it was done a-purpose! Reminds me of piece day at school. There was a mighty pretty piece I learned called the 'Wreck of the Asperus.'" And she subsided into a genteel melancholy.

I saw that Mr. Mifflin was well astride his hobby: he had started to tell the children about Robin Hood, but I had the sense to give him a wink. We had to be getting along or surely Andrew might be on us. So while Mifflin was putting Pegasus into the shafts again I picked out seven or eight books that I thought would fit the needs of the Masons. Mr. Mason insisted that "Happiness and Hayseed" be included among them, and gave me a crisp five-dollar bill, refusing any change. "No, no," he said, "I've had more fun than I get at a grange meeting. Come round again, Miss McGill; I'm going to tell Andrew what a good show this travelling theayter of yours gives! And you, Professor, any time you're here about road-mending season, stop in an' tell me some more good advice. Well, I must get back to the field."

Bock fell in under the van, and we creaked off down the lane. Mifflin filled his pipe and was chuckling to himself. I was a little worried now for fear Andrew might overtake us.

"It's a wonder Sam Mason didn't call up Andrew," I said. "It must have looked mighty queer to him for an old farm hand like me to be around, peddling books."

"He would have done it straight off," said Mifflin, "but you see, I cut his telephone wire!"

Chapter 5

I gazed in astonishment at the wizened little rogue. Here was a new side to the amiable idealist! Apparently there was a streak of fearless deviltry in him besides his gentle love of books. I'm bound to say that now, for the first time, I really admired him. I had burnt my own very respectable boats behind me, and I rather enjoyed knowing that he, too, could act briskly in a pinch.

"Well!" I said. "You are a cool hand! It's a good job for you that you didn't stay a schoolmaster. You might have taught your pupils some fine deviltries! And at your age, too!"

I'm afraid my raillery goes a little too far sometimes. He flushed a bit at my reference to his age, and puffed sharply at his pipe.

"I say," he rejoined, "how old do you think I am, anyway? Only forty-one, by the bones of Byron! Henry VIII was only forty-one when he married Anne Boleyn. There are many consolations in history for people over forty! Remember that when you get there.

"Shakespeare wrote 'King Lear' at forty-one," he added, more humorously; and then burst out laughing. "I'd like to edit a series of 'Chloroform Classics,' to include only books written after forty. Who was that doctor man who recommended anaesthetics for us at that age? Now isn't that just like a medico? Nurse us through the diseases of childhood, and as soon as we settle down into permanent good health and worldly wisdom, and freedom from doctors' fees, why he loses interest in us! Jove! I must note that down and bring it into my book."

He pulled out a memorandum book and jotted down "Chloroform
Classics" in a small, neat hand.

"Well," I said (I felt a little contrite, as I was sincerely sorry to have offended him), "I've passed forty myself in some measurements, so youth no longer has any terrors for me."

He looked at me rather comically.

"My dear madam," he said, "your age is precisely eighteen. I think that if we escape the clutches of the Sage of Redfield you may really begin to live."

"Oh, Andrew's not a bad sort," I said. "He's absentminded, and hot tempered, and a little selfish. The publishers have done their best to spoil him, but for a literary man I guess he's quite human. He rescued me from being a governess, and that's to his credit. If only he didn't take his meals quite so much as a matter of course...."

"The preposterous thing about him is that he really can *write*," said Mifflin. "I envy him that. Don't let him know I said so, but as a matter of fact his prose is almost as good as Thoreau. He approaches facts as daintily as a cat crossing a wet road."

"You should see him at dinner," I thought; or rather I meant to think it, but the words slipped out. I found myself thinking aloud in a rather disconcerting way while sitting with this strange little person.

He looked at me. I noticed for the first time that his eyes were slate blue, with funny birds' foot wrinkles at the corners.

"That's so," he said. "I never thought of that. A fine prose style certainly presupposes sound nourishment. Excellent point that... And yet Thoreau did his own cooking. A sort of Boy Scout I guess, with a badge as kitchen master. Perhaps he took Beechnut bacon with him into the woods. I wonder who cooked for Stevenson—Cummy? The 'Child's Garden of Verses' was really a kind of kitchen garden, wasn't it? I'm afraid the commissariat problem has weighed rather heavily on you. I'm glad you've got away from it."

All this was getting rather intricate for me. I set it down as I remember it, inaccurately perhaps. My governess days are pretty far astern now, and my line is common sense rather than literary allusions. I said something of the sort.

"Common sense?" he repeated. "Good Lord, ma'am, sense is the most uncommon thing in the world. I haven't got it. I don't believe your brother has, from what you say. Bock here has it. See how he trots along the road, keeps an eye on the scenery, and minds his own business. I never saw him get into a fight yet. Wish I could say the same of myself. I named him after Boccaccio, to remind me to read the 'Decameron' some day."

"Judging by the way you talk," I said, "you ought to be quite a writer yourself."

"Talkers never write. They go on talking."

There was a considerable silence. Mifflin relit his pipe and watched the landscape with a shrewd eye. I held the reins loosely, and Peg ambled along with a steady clop-clop. Parnassus creaked musically, and the mid-afternoon sun lay rich across the road. We passed another farm, but I did not suggest stopping as I felt we ought to push on. Mifflin seemed lost in meditation, and I began to wonder, a little uneasily, how the adventure would turn out. This quaintly masterful little man was a trifle disconcerting. Across the next ridge I could see the Greenbriar church spire shining white.

"Do you know this part of the country?" I asked finally.

"Not this exact section. I've been in Port Vigor often, but then I was on the road that runs along the Sound. I suppose this village ahead is Greenbriar?"

"Yes," I said. "It's about thirteen miles from there to Port   Vigor. How do you expect to get back to Brooklyn?"

"Oh, Brooklyn?" he said vaguely. "Yes, I'd forgotten about Brooklyn for the minute. I was thinking of my book. Why, I guess I'll take the train from Port Vigor. The trouble is, you can never get to Brooklyn without going through New York. It's symbolic, I suppose."

Again there was a silence. Finally he said, "Is there another town between Greenbriar and Port Vigor?"

"Yes, Shelby," I said. "About five miles from Greenbriar."

"That'll be as far as you'll get to-night," he said. "I'll see you safe to Shelby, and then make tracks for Port Vigor. I hope there's a decent inn at Shelby where you can stop overnight."

I hoped so, too, but I wasn't going to let him see that with the waning afternoon my enthusiasm was a little less robust. I was wondering what Andrew was thinking, and whether Mrs. McNally had left things in good order. Like most Swedes she had to be watched or she left her work only three quarters done. And I didn't depend any too much on her daughter Rosie to do the housework efficiently. I wondered what kind of meals Andrew would get. And probably he would go right on wearing his summer underclothes, although I had already reminded him about changing. Then there were the chickens...

Well, the Rubicon was crossed now, and there was nothing to be done.

To my surprise, little Redbeard had divined my anxiety. "Now don't you worry about the Sage," he said kindly. "A man that draws his royalties isn't going to starve. By the bones of John Murray, his publishers can send him a cook if necessary! This is a holiday for you, and don't you forget it."

And with this cheering sentiment in my mind, we rolled sedately down the hill toward Greenbriar.

I am about as hardy as most folks, I think, but I confess I balked a little at the idea of facing the various people I know in Greenbriar as the owner of a bookvan and the companion of a literary huckster. Also I recollected that if Andrew should try to trace us it would be as well for me to keep out of sight. So after telling Mr. Mifflin how I felt about matters I dived into the Parnassus and lay down most comfortably on the bunk. Bock the terrier joined me, and I rested there in great comfort of mind and body as we ambled down the grade. The sun shone through the little skylight gilding a tin pan that hung over the cook stove. Tacked here and there were portraits of authors, and I noticed a faded newspaper cutting pinned up. The headlines ran: "Literary Pedlar Lectures on Poetry." I read it through. Apparently the Professor (so I had begun to call him, as the aptness of the nickname stuck in my mind) had given a lecture in Camden, N.J., where he had asserted that Tennyson was a greater poet than Walt Whitman; and the boosters of the Camden poet had enlivened the evening with missiles. It seems that the chief Whitman disciple in Camden is Mr. Traubel; and Mr. Mifflin had started the rumpus by asserting that Tennyson, too, had "Traubels of his own." What an absurd creature the Professor was, I thought, as I lay comfortably lulled by the rolling wheels.

Greenbriar is a straggling little town, built around a large common meadow. Mifflin's general plan in towns, he had told me, was to halt Parnassus in front of the principal store or hotel, and when a little throng had gathered he would put up the flaps of the van, distribute his cards, and deliver a harangue on the value of good books. I lay concealed inside, but I gathered from the sounds that this was what was happening. We came to a stop; I heard a growing murmur of voices and laughter outside, and then the click of the raised sides of the wagon. I heard Mifflin's shrill, slightly nasal voice making facetious remarks as he passed out the cards. Evidently Bock was quite accustomed to the routine, for though his tail wagged gently when the Professor began to talk, he lay quite peaceably dozing at my feet.

"My friends," said Mr. Mifflin. "You remember Abe Lincoln's joke about the dog? If you call a tail a leg, said Abe, how many legs has a dog? Five, you answer. No, says Abe; because calling a tail a leg doesn't make it a leg. Well, there are lots of us in the same case as that dog's tail. Calling us men doesn't *make* us men. No creature on earth has a right to think himself a human being if he doesn't know at least one good book. The man that spends every evening chewing Piper Heidsieck at the store is unworthy to catch the intimations of a benevolent Creator. The man that's got a few good books on his shelf is making his wife happy, giving his children a square deal, and he's likely to be a better citizen himself. How about that, parson?"

I heard the deep voice of Reverend Kane, the Methodist minister: "You're dead right, Professor!" he shouted. "Tell us some more about books. I'm right with you!" Evidently Mr. Kane had been attracted by the sight of Parnassus, and I could hear him muttering to himself as he pulled one or two books from the shelves. How surprised he would have been if he had known I was inside the van! I took the precaution of slipping the bolt of the door at the back, and drew the curtains. Then I crept back into the bunk. I began to imagine what an absurd situation there would be if Andrew should arrive on the scene.

"You are all used to hucksters and pedlars and fellows selling every kind of junk from brooms to bananas," said the Professor's voice. "But how often does any one come round here to sell you books? You've got your town library, I dare say; but there are some books that folks ought to own. I've got 'em all here from Bibles to cook books. They'll speak for themselves. Step up to the shelves, friends, and pick and choose."

I heard the parson asking the price of something he had found on the shelves, and I believe he bought it; but the hum of voices around the flanks of Parnassus was very soothing, and in spite of my interest in what was going on I'm afraid I fell asleep. I must have been pretty tired; anyway I never felt the van start again. The Professor says he looked in through the little window from the driver's seat, and saw me sound asleep. And the next thing I knew I woke up with a start to find myself rolling leisurely in the dark. Bock was still lying over my feet, and there was a faint, musical clang from the bucket under the van which struck against something now and then. The Professor was sitting in front, with a lighted lantern hanging from the peak of the van roof. He was humming some outlandish song to himself, with a queer, monotonous refrain:

Shipwrecked was I off Soft Perowse
  And right along the shore,
And so I did resolve to roam
  The country to explore.
Tommy rip fal lal and a balum tip
  Tommy rip fal lal I dee;
And so I did resolve to roam
  The country for to see!

I jumped out of the bunk, cracked my shins against something, and uttered a rousing halloo. Parnassus stopped, and the Professor pushed back the sliding window behind the driver's seat.

"Heavens!" I said. "Father Time, what o'clock is it?"

"Pretty near supper time, I reckon. You must have fallen asleep while I was taking money from the Philistines. I made nearly three dollars for you. Let's pull up along the road and have a bite to eat."

He guided Pegasus to one side of the road, and then showed me how to light the swinging lamp that hung under the skylight. "No use to light the stove on a lovely evening like this," he said. "I'll collect some sticks and we can cook outside. You get out your basket of grub and I'll make a fire." He unhitched Pegasus, tied her to a tree, and gave her a nose bag of oats. Then he rooted around for some twigs and had a fire going in a jiffy. In five minutes I had bacon and scrambled eggs sizzling in a frying pan, and he had brought out a pail of water from the cooler under the bunk, and was making tea.

I never enjoyed a picnic so much! It was a perfect autumn evening, windless and frosty, with a dead black sky and a tiny rim of new moon like a thumb-nail paring. We had our eggs and bacon, washed down with tea and condensed milk, and followed by bread and jam. The little fire burned blue and cozy, and we sat on each side of it while Bock scoured the pan and ate the crusts.

"This your own bread, Miss McGill?" he asked.

"Yes," I said. "I was calculating the other day that I've baked more than 400 loaves a year for the last fifteen years. That's more than 6,000 loaves of bread. They can put that on my tombstone."

"The art of baking bread is as transcendent a mystery as the art of making sonnets," said Redbeard. "And then your hot biscuits—they might be counted as shorter lyrics, I suppose—triolets perhaps. That makes quite an anthology, or a doxology, if you prefer it."

"Yeast is yeast, and West is West," I said, and was quite surprised at my own cleverness. I hadn't made a remark like that to Andrew in five years.

"I see you are acquainted with Kipling," he said.

"Oh, yes, every governess is."

"Where and whom did you govern?"

"I was in New York, with the family of a wealthy stockbroker. There were three children. I used to take them walking in Central Park."

"Did you ever go to Brooklyn?" he asked abruptly.

"Never," I replied.

"Ah!" he said. "That's just the trouble. New York is Babylon; Brooklyn is the true Holy City. New York is the city of envy, office work, and hustle; Brooklyn is the region of homes and happiness. It is extraordinary: poor, harassed New Yorkers presume to look down on low-lying, home-loving Brooklyn, when as a matter of fact it is the precious jewel their souls are thirsting for and they never know it. Broadway: think how symbolic the name is. Broad is the way that leadeth to destruction! But in Brooklyn the ways are narrow, and they lead to the Heavenly City of content. Central Park: there you are— the centre of things, hemmed in by walls of pride. Now how much better is Prospect Park, giving a fair view over the hills of humility! There is no hope for New Yorkers, for they glory in their skyscraping sins; but in Brooklyn there is the wisdom of the lowly."

"So you think that if I had been a governess in Brooklyn I should have been so contented that I would never have come with Andrew and compiled my anthology of 6,000 loaves of bread and the lesser lyrics?"

But the volatile Professor had already soared to other points of view, and was not to be thwarted by argument.

"Of course Brooklyn is a dingy place, really," he admitted. "But to me it symbolizes a state of mind, whereas New York is only a state of pocket. You see I was a boy in Brooklyn: it still trails clouds of glory for me. When I get back there and start work on my book I shall be as happy as Nebuchadnezzar when he left off grass and returned to tea and crumpets. 'Literature Among the Farmers' I'm going to call it, but that's a poor title. I'd like to read you some of my notes for it."

I'm afraid I poorly concealed a yawn. As a matter of fact I was sleepy, and it was growing chilly.

"Tell me first," I said, "where in the world are we, and what time is it?"

He pulled out a turnip watch. "It's nine o'clock," he said, "and we're about two miles from Shelby, I should reckon. Perhaps we'd better get along. They told me in Greenbriar that the Grand Central Hotel in Shelby is a good place to stop at. That's why I wasn't anxious to get there. It sounds so darned like New York."

He bundled the cooking utensils back into Parnassus, hitched Peg up again, and tied Bock to the stern of the van. Then he insisted on giving me the two dollars and eighty cents he had collected in Greenbriar. I was really too sleepy to protest, and of course it was mine anyway. We creaked off along the dark and silent road between the pine woods. I think he talked fluently about his pilgrim's progress among the farmers of a dozen states, but (to be honest) I fell asleep in my corner of the seat. I woke up when we halted before the one hotel in Shelby—a plain, unimposing country inn, despite its absurd name. I left him to put Parnassus and the animals away for the night, while I engaged a room. Just as I got my key from the clerk he came into the dingy lobby.

"Well, Mr. Mifflin," I said. "Shall I see you in the morning?"

"I had intended to push on to Port Vigor to-night," he said, "but as it's fully eight miles (they tell me), I guess I'll bivouac here. I think I'll go into the smoking-room and put them wise to some good books. We won't say good-bye till to-morrow."

My room was pleasant and clean (fairly so). I took my suit case up with me and had a hot bath. As I fell asleep I heard a shrill voice ascending from below, punctuated with masculine laughter. The Pilgrim was making   more   converts!

Chapter 6

I had a curious feeling of bewilderment when I woke the next morning. The bare room with the red-and-blue rag carpet and green china toilet set was utterly strange. In the hall outside I heard a clock strike. "Heavens!" I thought, "I've overslept myself nearly two hours. What on earth will Andrew do for breakfast?" And then as I ran to close the window I saw the blue Parnassus with its startling red letters standing in the yard. Instantly I remembered. And discreetly peeping from behind the window shade I saw that the Professor, armed with a tin of paint, was blotting out his own name on the side of the van, evidently intending to substitute mine. That was something I had not thought of. However, I might as well make the best of it.

I dressed promptly, repacked my bag, and hurried downstairs for breakfast. The long table was nearly empty, but one or two men sitting at the other end eyed me curiously. Through the window I could see my name in large, red letters, growing on the side of the van, as the Professor diligently wielded his brush. And when I had finished my coffee and beans and bacon I noticed with some amusement that the Professor had painted out the line about Shakespeare, Charles Lamb, and so on, and had substituted new lettering. The sign now read:

**H. MCGILL'S TRAVELLING PARNASSUS GOOD BOOKS
FOR SALE COOK BOOKS A SPECIALTY INQUIRE
WITHIN**

Evidently he distrusted my familiarity with the classics.

I paid my bill at the desk, and was careful also to pay the charge for putting up the horse and van overnight. Then I strolled into the stable yard, where I found Mr. Mifflin regarding his handiwork with satisfaction. He had freshened up all the red lettering, which shone brilliantly in the morning sunlight.

"Good-morning," I said.

He returned it.

"There!" he cried—"Parnassus is really yours! All the world lies before you! And I've got some more money for you. I sold some books last night. I persuaded the hotel keeper to buy several volumes of O. Henry for his smoking-room shelf, and I sold the 'Waldorf Cook Book' to the cook. My! wasn't her coffee awful? I hope the cook book will better it."

He handed me two limp bills and a handful of small change. I took it gravely and put it in my purse. This was really not bad—more than ten dollars in less than twenty-four hours.

"Parnassus seems to be a gold mine," I said.

"Which way do you think you'll go?" he asked.

"Well, as I know you want to get to Port Vigor I might just as well give you a lift that way," I answered.

"Good! I was hoping you'd say that. They tell me the stage for Port Vigor doesn't leave till noon, and I think it would kill me to hang around here all morning with no books to sell. Once I get on the train I'll be all right."

Bock was tied up in a corner of the yard, under the side door of the hotel. I went over to release him while the Professor was putting Peg into harness. As I stooped to unfasten the chain from his collar I heard some one talking through the telephone. The hotel lobby was just over my head, and the window was open.

"What did you say?"

"_____ _____ _____ _____"

"McGill? Yes, sir, registered here last night. She's here now."

I didn't wait to hear more. Unfastening Bock, I hurried to tell Mifflin. His eyes sparkled.

"The Sage is evidently on our spoor," he chuckled. "Well, let's be off. I don't see what he can do even if he overhauls us."

The clerk was calling me from the window: "Miss McGill, your brother's on the wire and asks to speak to you."

"Tell him I'm busy," I retorted, and climbed onto the seat. It was not a diplomatic reply, I'm afraid, but I was too exhilarated by the keen morning and the spirit of adventure to stop to think of a better answer. Mifflin clucked to Peg, and off we went.

The road from Shelby to Port Vigor runs across the broad hill slopes that trend toward the Sound; and below, on our left, the river lay glittering in the valley. It was a perfect landscape: the woods were all bronze and gold; the clouds were snowy white and seemed like heavenly washing hung out to air; the sun was warm and swam gloriously in an arch of superb blue. My heart was uplifted indeed. For the first time, I think, I knew how Andrew feels on those vagabond trips of his. Why had all this been hidden from me before? Why had the transcendent mystery of baking bread blinded me so long to the mysteries of sun and sky and wind in the trees? We passed a white farmhouse close to the road. By the gate sat the farmer on a log, whittling a stick and smoking his pipe. Through the kitchen window I could see a woman blacking the stove. I wanted to cry out: "Oh, silly woman! Leave your stove, your pots and pans and chores, even if only for one day! Come out and see the sun in the sky and the river in the distance!" The farmer looked blankly at Parnassus as we passed, and then I remembered my mission as a distributor of literature. Mifflin was sitting with one foot on his bulging portmanteau, watching the tree tops rocking in the cool wind. He seemed to be far away in a morning muse. I threw down the reins and accosted the farmer.

"Good-morning, friend."

"Morning to you, ma'am," he said firmly.

"I'm selling books," I said. "I wonder if there isn't something you need?"

"Thanks, lady," he said, "but I bought a mort o' books last year an' I don't believe I'll ever read 'em this side Jordan. A whole set o' 'Funereal Orations' what an agent left on me at a dollar a month. I could qualify as earnest mourner at any death-bed merrymakin' now, I reckon."

"You need some books to teach you how to live, not how to die," I said. "How about your wife—wouldn't she enjoy a good book? How about some fairy tales for the children?"

"Bless me," he said, "I ain't got a wife. I never was a daring man, and I guess I'll confine my melancholy pleasures to them funereal orators for some time yet."

"Well, now, hold on a minute!" I exclaimed. "I've got just the thing for you." I had been looking over the shelves with some care, and remembered seeing a copy of "Reveries of a Bachelor." I clambered down, raised the flap of the van (it gave me quite a thrill to do it myself for the first time), and hunted out the book. I looked inside the cover and saw the letters *n m* in Mifflin's neat hand.

"Here you are," I said. "I'll sell you that for thirty cents."

"Thank you kindly, ma'am," he said courteously. "But honestly I wouldn't know what to do with it. I am working through a government report on scabworm and fungus, and I sandwich in a little of them funereal speeches with it, and honestly that's about all the readin' I figure on. That an' the Port Vigor Clarion."

I saw that he really meant it, so I climbed back on the seat. I would have liked to talk to the woman in the kitchen who was peering out of the window in amazement, but I decided it would be better to jog on and not waste time. The farmer and I exchanged friendly salutes, and Parnassus rumbled on.

The morning was so lovely that I did not feel talkative, and as the Professor seemed pensive I said nothing. But as Peg plodded slowly up a gentle slope he suddenly pulled a book out of his pocket and began to read aloud. I was watching the river, and did not turn round, but listened carefully:

"Rolling cloud, volleying wind, and wheeling sun—the blue tabernacle of sky, the circle of the seasons, the sparkling multitude of the stars—all these are surely part of one rhythmic, mystic whole. Everywhere, as we go about our small business, we must discern the fingerprints of the gigantic plan, the orderly and inexorable routine with neither beginning nor end, in which death is but a preface to another birth, and birth the certain forerunner of another death. We human beings are as powerless to conceive the motive or the moral of it all as the dog is powerless to understand the reasoning in his master's mind. He sees the master's acts, benevolent or malevolent, and wags his tail. But the master's acts are always inscrutable to him. And so with us.

"And therefore, brethren, let us take the road with a light heart. Let us praise the bronze of the leaves and the crash of the surf while we have eyes to see and ears to hear. An honest amazement at the unspeakable beauties of the world is a comely posture for the scholar. Let us all be scholars under Mother Nature's eye.

"How do you like that?" he asked.

"A little heavy, but very good," I said. "There's nothing in it about the transcendent mystery of baking bread!"

He looked rather blank.

"Do you know who wrote it?" he asked.

I made a valiant effort to summon some of my governessly recollections of literature.

"I give it up," I said feebly. "Is it Carlyle?"

"That is by Andrew McGill," he said. "One of his cosmic passages which are now beginning to be reprinted in schoolbooks. The blighter writes well."

I began to be uneasy lest I should be put through a literary catechism, so I said nothing, but roused Peg into an amble. To tell the truth I was more curious to hear the Professor talk about his own book than about Andrew's. I had always carefully refrained from reading Andrew's stuff, as I thought it rather dull.

"As for me," said the Professor, "I have no facility at the grand style. I have always suffered from the feeling that it's better to read a good book than to write a poor one; and I've done so much mixed reading in my time that my mind is full of echoes and voices of better men. But this book I'm worrying about now really deserves to be written, I think, for it has a message of its own."

He gazed almost wistfully across the sunny valley. In the distance I caught a glint of the Sound. The Professor's faded tweed cap was slanted over one ear, and his stubby little beard shone bright red in the sun. I kept a sympathetic silence. He seemed pleased to have some one to talk to about his precious book.

"The world is full of great writers about literature," he said, "but they're all selfish and aristocratic. Addison, Lamb, Hazlitt, Emerson, Lowell—take any one you choose—they all conceive the love of books as a rare and perfect mystery for the few—a thing of the secluded study where they can sit alone at night with a candle, and a cigar, and a glass of port on the table and a spaniel on the hearthrug. What I say is, who has ever gone out into high roads and hedges to bring literature home to the plain man? To bring it home to his business and bosom, as somebody says? The farther into the country you go, the fewer and worse books you find. I've spent several years joggling around with this citadel of crime, and by the bones of Ben Ezra I don't think I ever found a really good book (except the Bible) at a farmhouse yet, unless I put it there myself. The mandarins of culture— what do they do to teach the common folk to read? It's no good writing down lists of books for farmers and compiling five-foot shelves; you've got to go out and visit the people yourself—take the books to them, talk to the teachers and bully the editors of country newspapers and farm magazines and tell the children stories—and then little by little you begin to get good books circulating in the veins of the nation. It's a great work, mind you! It's like carrying the Holy Grail to some of these way-back farmhouses. And I wish there were a thousand Parnassuses instead of this one. I'd never give it up if it weren't for my book: but I want to write about my ideas in the hope of stirring other folk up, too. I don't suppose there's a publisher in the country will take it!"

"Try Mr. Decameron," I said. "He's always been very nice to Andrew."

"Think what it would mean," he cried, waving an eloquent hand, "if some rich man would start a fund to equip a hundred or so wagons like this to go huckstering literature around through the rural districts. It would pay, too, once you got started. Yes, by the bones of Webster! I went to a meeting of booksellers once, at some hotel in New York, and told 'em about my scheme. They laughed at me. But I've had more fun toting books around in this Parnassus than I could have had in fifty years sitting in a bookstore, or teaching school, or preaching. Life's full of savour when you go creaking along the road like this. Look at today, with the sun and the air and the silver clouds. Best of all, though, I love the rainy days. I used to pull up alongside the road, throw a rubber blanket over Peg, and Bock and I would curl up in the bunk and smoke and read. I used to read aloud to Bock: we went through 'Midshipman Easy' together, and a good deal of Shakespeare. He's a very bookish dog. We've seen some queer experiences in this Parnassus."

The hill road from Shelby to Port Vigor is a lonely one, as most of the farmhouses lie down in the valley. If I had known better we might have taken the longer and more populous way, but as a matter of fact I was enjoying the wide view and the solitary road lying white in the sunshine. We jogged along very pleasantly. Once more we stopped at a house where Mifflin pleaded for a chance to exercise his art. I was much amused when he succeeded in selling a copy of "Grimm's Fairy Tales" to a shrewish spinster on the plea that she would enjoy reading the stories to her nephews and nieces who were coming to visit her.

"My!" he chuckled, as he gave me the dingy quarter he had extracted. "There's nothing in that book as grim as she is!"

A little farther on we halted by a roadside spring to give Peg a drink, and I suggested lunch. I had laid in some bread and cheese in Shelby, and with this and some jam we made excellent sandwiches. As we were sitting by the fence the motor stage trundled past on its way to Port Vigor. A little distance down the road it halted, and then went on again. I saw a familiar figure walking back toward us.

"Now I'm in for it," I said to the Professor. "Here's Andrew!"

Chapter 7

Andrew is just as thin as I am fat, and his clothes hang on him in the most comical way. He is very tall and shambling, wears a ragged beard and a broad Stetson hat, and suffers amazingly from hay fever in the autumn. (In fact, his essay on "Hay Fever" is the best thing he ever wrote, I think.) As he came striding up the road I noticed how his trousers fluttered at the ankles as the wind plucked at them. The breeze curled his beard back under his chin and his face was quite dark with anger. I couldn't help being amused; he looked so funny.

"The Sage looks like Bernard Shaw," whispered Mifflin.

I always believe in drawing first blood.

"Good-morning, Andrew," I called cheerfully. "Want to buy any books?" I halted Pegasus, and Andrew stood a little in front of the wheel—partly out of breath and mostly out of temper.

"What on earth is this nonsense, Helen?" he said angrily. "You've led me the deuce of a chase since yesterday. And who is this—this person you're driving with?"

"Andrew," I said, "you forget your manners. Let me introduce Mr. Mifflin. I have bought his caravan and am taking a holiday, selling books. Mr. Mifflin is on his way to Port Vigor where he takes the train to Brooklyn."

Andrew stared at the Professor without speaking. I could tell by the blaze in his light-blue eyes that he was thoroughly angry, and I feared things would be worse before they were better. Andrew is slow to wrath, but a very hard person to deal with when roused. And I had some inkling by this time of the Professor's temperament. Moreover, I am afraid that some of my remarks had rather prejudiced him against Andrew, as a brother at any rate and apart from his excellent prose.

Mifflin had the next word. He had taken off his funny little cap, and his bare skull shone like an egg. I noticed a little sort of fairy ring of tiny drops around his crown.

"My dear sir," said Mifflin, "the proceedings look somewhat unusual, but the facts are simple to narrate. Your sister has bought this van and its contents, and I have been instructing her in my theories of the dissemination of good books. You as a literary man..."

Andrew paid absolutely no attention to the Professor, and I saw a slow flush tinge Mifflin's sallow cheek.

"Look here, Helen," said Andrew, "do you think I propose to have my sister careering around the State with a strolling vagabond? Upon my soul you ought to have better sense—and at your age and weight! I got home yesterday and found your ridiculous note. I went to Mrs. Collins, and she knew nothing. I went to Mason's, and found him wondering who had bilked his telephone. I suppose you did that. He had seen this freight car of yours and put me on the track. But my God! I never thought to see a woman of forty abducted by gypsies!"

Mifflin was about to speak but I waved him back.

"Now see here Andrew," I said, "you talk too quickly. A woman of forty (you exaggerate, by the way) who has compiled an anthology of 6,000 loaves of bread and dedicated it to you deserves some courtesy. When *you* want to run off on some vagabond tour or other you don't hesitate to do it. You expect me to stay home and do the Lady Eglantine in the poultry yard. By the ghost of Susan B. Anthony, I won't do it! This is the first real holiday I've had in fifteen years, and I'm going to suit myself."

Andrew's mouth opened, but I shook my fist so convincingly that he halted.

"I bought this Parnassus from Mr. Mifflin fair and square for four hundred dollars. That's the price of about thirteen hundred dozen eggs," I said. (I had worked this out in my head while Mifflin was talking about his book.)

"The money's mine, and I'm going to use it my own way. Now, Andrew McGill, if you want to buy any books, you can parley with me. Otherwise, I'm on my way. You can expect me back when you see me." I handed him one of Mifflin's little cards, which were in a pocket at the side of the van, and gathered up the reins. I was really angry, for Andrew had been both unreasonable and insulting.

Andrew looked at the card, and tore it in halves. He looked at the side of Parnassus where the fresh red lettering was still damp.

"Well, upon my word," he said, "you must be crazy." He burst into a violent fit of sneezing—a last touch of hay fever, I suspect, as there was still goldenrod in the meadows. He coughed and sneezed furiously, which made him madder than ever. At last he turned to Mifflin who was sitting bald-headed with a flushed face and very bright eyes. Andrew took him all in, the shabby Norfolk jacket, the bulging memorandum book in his pocket, the stuffed portmanteau under his foot, even the copy of "Happiness and Hayseed" which had dropped to the floor and lay back up.

"Look here, you," said Andrew, "I don't know by what infernal arts you cajoled my sister away to go vagabonding in a huckster's wagon, but I know this, that if you've cheated her out of her money I'll have the law on you."

I tried to insert a word of protest, but matters had gone too far. The Professor was as mad as Andrew now.

"By the bones of Piers Plowman," he said, "I had expected to meet a man of letters and the author of this book"—he held up "Happiness and Hayseed"—"but I see I was mistaken. I tell you, sir, a man who would insult his sister before a stranger, as you have done, is an oaf and a cad." He threw the book over the hedge, and before I could say a word he had vaulted over the off wheel and ran round behind the van.

"Look here sir," he said, with his little red beard bristling, "your sister is over age and acting of her own free will. By the bones of the Baptist, I don't blame her for wanting a vacation if this is the way you treat her. She is nothing to me, sir, and I am nothing to her, but I propose to be a teacher to you. Put up your hands and I'll give you a lesson!"

This was too much for me. I believe I screamed aloud, and started to clamber from the van. But before I could do anything the two fanatics had begun to pummel each other. I saw Andrew swing savagely at Mifflin, and Mifflin hit him square on the chin. Andrew's hat fell on the road. Peg stood placidly, and Bock made as if to grab Andrew's leg, but I hopped out and seized him.

It was certainly a weird sight. I suppose I should have wrung my hands and had hysterics, but as a matter of fact I was almost amused, it was so silly. Thank goodness the road was deserted.

Andrew was a foot taller than the Professor, but awkward, loosely knit, and unmuscular, while the little Redbeard was wiry as a cat. Also Andrew was so furious that he was quite beside himself, and Mifflin was in the cold anger that always wins. Andrew landed a couple of flailing blows on the other man's chest and shoulders, but in thirty seconds he got another punch on the chin followed by one on the nose that tumbled him over backward.

Andrew sat in the road fishing for a handkerchief, and Mifflin stood glaring at him, but looking very ill at ease. Neither of them said a word. Bock broke away from me and capered and danced about Mifflin's feet as if it were all a game. It was an extraordinary scene.

Andrew got up, mopping his bleeding nose.

"Upon my soul," he said, "I almost respect you for that punch. But by Jove I'll have the law on you for kidnapping my sister. You're a fine kind of a pirate."

Mifflin said nothing.

"Don't be a fool, Andrew" I said. "Can't you see that I want a little adventure of my own? Go home and bake six thousand loaves of bread, and by the time they're done I'll be back again. I think two men of your age ought to be ashamed of yourselves. I'm going off to sell books." And with that I climbed up to the seat and clucked to Pegasus. Andrew and Mifflin and Bock remained standing in the road.

I was mad all the way through. I was mad at both men for behaving like schoolboys. I was mad at Andrew for being so unreasonable, yet in a way I admired him for it; I was mad at Mifflin for giving Andrew a bloody nose, and yet I appreciated the spirit in which it was done. I was mad at myself for causing all the trouble, and I was mad at Parnassus. If there had been a convenient cliff handy I would have pushed the old thing over it. But now I was in for it, and just had to go on. Slowly I rolled up a long grade, and then saw Port Vigor lying ahead and the broad blue stretches of the Sound.

Parnassus rumbled on with its pleasant creak, and the mellow sun and sweep of the air soon soothed me. I began to taste salt in the wind, and above the meadows two or three seagulls were circling. Like all women, my angry mood melted into a reaction of exaggerated tenderness and I began to praise both Andrew and Mifflin in my heart. How fine to have a brother so solicitous of his sister's welfare and reputation! And yet, how splendid the little, scrawny Professor had been! How quick to resent an insult and how bold to avenge it! His absurd little tweed cap was lying on the seat, and I picked it up almost sentimentally. The lining was frayed and torn. From my suit case in the van I got out a small sewing kit, and hanging the reins on a hook I began to stitch up the rents as Peg jogged along. I thought with amusement of the quaint life Mr. Mifflin had led in his "caravan of culture." I imagined him addressing the audience of Whitman disciples in Camden, and wondered how the fuss ended. I imagined him in his beloved Brooklyn, strolling in Prospect Park and preaching to chance comers his gospel of good books. How different was his militant love of literature from Andrew's quiet satisfaction. And yet how much they really had in common! It tickled me to think of Mifflin reading aloud from "Happiness and Hayseed," and praising it so highly, just before fighting with the author and giving him a bloody nose. I remembered that I should have spoken to Andrew about feeding the hens, and reminded him of his winter undergarments. What helpless creatures men are, after all!

I finished mending the cap in high good humour.

I had hardly laid it down when I heard a quick step in the road behind me, and looking back, there was Mifflin, striding along with his bald pate covered with little beads of moisture. Bock trotted sedately at his heels. I halted Peg.

"Well," I said, "what's happened to Andrew?"

The Professor still looked a bit shamefaced. "The Sage is a tenacious person," he said. "We argued for a bit without much satisfaction. As a matter of fact we nearly came to blows again, only he got another waft of goldenrod, which started him sneezing, and then his nose began bleeding once more. He is convinced that I'm a ruffian, and said so in excellent prose. Honestly, I admire him a great deal. I believe he intends to have the law on me. I gave him my Brooklyn address in case he wants to follow the matter up. I think I rather pleased him by asking him to autograph 'Happiness and Hayseed' for me. I found it lying in the ditch."

"Well," I said, "you two are certainly a great pair of lunatics. You both ought to go on the stage. You'd be as good as Weber and Fields. Did he give you the autograph?"

He pulled the book out of his pocket. Scrawled in it in pencil were the words "I have shed blood for Mr. Mifflin. Andrew McGill."

"I shall read the book again with renewed interest," said   Mifflin.
"May I get in?"

"By all means," I said. "There's Port Vigor in front of us."

He put on his cap, noticed that it seemed to feel different, pulled it off again, and then looked at me in a quaint embarrassment.

"You are very good, Miss McGill," he said.

"Where did Andrew go?" I asked.

"He set off for Shelby on foot," Mifflin answered. "He has a grand stride for walking. He suddenly remembered that he had left some potatoes boiling on the fire yesterday afternoon, and said he must get back to attend to them. He said he hoped you would send him a postal card now and then. Do you know, he reminds me of Thoreau more than ever."

"He reminds me of a burnt cooking pot," I said. "I suppose all my kitchenware will be in a horrible state when   I   get   home."

Chapter 8

Port Vigor is a fascinating old town. It is built on a point jutting out into the Sound. Dimly in the distance one can see the end of Long Island, which Mifflin viewed with sparkling eyes. It seemed to bring him closer to Brooklyn. Several schooners were beating along the estuary in the fresh wind, and there was a delicious tang of brine in the air. We drove direct to the station where the Professor alighted. We took his portmanteau, and shut Bock inside the van to prevent the dog from following him. Then there was an awkward pause as he stood by the wheel with his cap off.

"Well, Miss McGill," he said, "there's an express train at five o'clock, so with luck I shall be in Brooklyn tonight. My brother's address is 600 Abingdon Avenue, and I hope when you're sending a card to the Sage you'll let me have one, too. I shall be very homesick for Parnassus, but I'd rather leave her with you than with any one I know."

He bowed very low, and before I could say a word he blew his nose violently and hurried away. I saw him carrying his valise into the station, and then he disappeared. I suppose that living alone with Andrew for all these years has unused me to the eccentricities of other people, but surely this little Redbeard was one of the strangest beings one would be likely to meet.

Bock yowled dismally inside, and I did not feel in any mood to sell books in Port Vigor. I drove back into the town and stopped at a tea shop for a pot of tea and some toast. When I came out I found that quite a little crowd had collected, partly owing to the strange appearance of Parnassus and partly because of Bock's plaintive cries from within. Most of the onlookers seemed to suspect the outfit of being part of a travelling menagerie, so almost against my will I put up the flaps, tied Bock to the tail of the wagon, and began to answer the humourous questions of the crowd. Two or three bought books without any urging, and it was some time before I could get away. Finally I shut up the van and pulled off, as I was afraid of seeing some one I knew. As I turned into the Woodbridge Road I heard the whistle of the five o'clock train to New York.

The twenty miles of road between Sabine Farm and Port Vigor was all familiar to me, but now to my relief I struck into a region that I had never visited. On my occasional trips to Boston I had always taken the train at Port Vigor, so the country roads were unknown. But I had set out on the Woodbridge way because Mifflin had spoken of a farmer, Mr. Pratt, who lived about four miles out of Port Vigor, on the Woodbridge Road. Apparently Mr. Pratt had several times bought books from the Professor and the latter had promised to visit him again. So I felt in duty bound to oblige a good customer.

After the varied adventures of the last two days it was almost a relief to be alone to think things over. Here was I, Helen McGill, in a queer case indeed. Instead of being home at Sabine Farm getting supper, I was trundling along a strange road, the sole owner of a Parnassus (probably the only one in existence), a horse, and a dog, and a cartload of books on my hands. Since the morning of the day before my whole life had twisted out of its accustomed orbit. I had spent four hundred dollars of my savings; I had sold about thirteen dollars' worth of books; I had precipitated a fight and met a philosopher.

Not only that, I was dimly beginning to evolve a new philosophy of my own. And all this in order to prevent Andrew from buying a lot more books! At any rate, I had been successful in that. When he had seen Parnassus at last, he had hardly looked at her—except in tones of scorn. I caught myself wondering whether the Professor would allude to the incident in his book, and hoping that he would send me a copy. But after all, why should he mention it? To him it was only one of a thousand adventures. As he had said angrily to Andrew, he was nothing to me, nor I to him. How could he realize that this was the first adventure I had had in the fifteen years I had been—what was it he called it?—compiling my anthology. Well, the funny little gingersnap!

I kept Bock tied to the back of the van, as I was afraid he might take a notion to go in search of his master. As we jogged on, and the falling sun cast a level light across the way, I got a bit lonely. This solitary vagabonding business was a bit sudden after fifteen years of home life. The road lay close to the water and I watched the Sound grow a deeper blue and then a dull purple. I could hear the surf pounding, and on the end of Long Island a far-away lighthouse showed a ruby spark. I thought of the little gingersnap roaring toward New York on the express, and wondered whether he was travelling in a Pullman or a day coach. A Pullman chair would feel easy after that hard Parnassus seat.

By and by we neared a farmhouse which I took to be Mr. Pratt's. It stood close to the road, with a big, red barn behind and a gilt weathervane representing a galloping horse. Curiously enough Peg seemed to recognize the place, for she turned in at the gate and neighed vigorously. It must have been a favourite stopping place for the Professor.

Through a lighted window I could see people sitting around a table. Evidently the Pratts were at supper. I drew up in the yard. Some one looked out of a window, and I heard a girl's voice:

"Why, Pa, here's Parnassus!"

Gingersnap must have been a welcome visitor at that farm, for in an instant the whole family turned out with a great scraping of chairs and clatter of dishes. A tall, sunburnt man, in a clean shirt with no collar, led the group, and then came a stout woman about my own build, and a hired man and three children.

"Good evening!" I said. "Is this Mr. Pratt?"

"Sure thing!" said he. "Where's the Perfessor?"

"On his way to Brooklyn," said I. "And I've got Parnassus. He told me to be sure to call on you. So here we are."

"Well, I want to know!" ejaculated Mrs. Pratt. "Think of Parnassus turned suffrage! Ben, you put up the critters, and I'll take Mrs. Mifflin in to supper."

"Hold on there," I said. "My name's McGill—Miss McGill. See, it's painted on the wagon. I bought the outfit from Mr. Mifflin. A business proposition entirely."

"Well, well," said Mr. Pratt. "We're glad to see any friend of the Perfessor. Sorry he's not here, too. Come right in and have a bite with us."

They were certainly good-hearted folk, Mr. and Mrs. Ben Pratt. He put Peg and Bock away in the barn and gave them their supper, while Mrs. Pratt took me up to her spare bedroom and brought me a jug of hot water. Then they all trooped back into the dining-room and the meal began again. I am a connoisseur of farm cooking, I guess, and I've got to hand it to Beulah Pratt that she was an A-1 housewife. Her hot biscuit was perfect; the coffee was real Mocha, simmered, not boiled; the cold sausage and potato salad was as good as any Andrew ever got. And she had a smoking-hot omelet sent in for me, and opened a pot of her own strawberry preserve.

The children (two boys and a girl) sat open-mouthed, nudging one another, and Mr. Pratt got out his pipe while I finished up on stewed pears and cream and chocolate cake. It was a regular meal. I wondered what Andrew was eating and whether he had found the nest behind the wood pile where the red hen always drops her eggs.

"Well, well," said Mr. Pratt, "tell us about the Perfessor. We was expectin' him here some time this fall. He generally gets here around cider time."

"I guess there isn't so much to tell," I said. "He stopped up at our place the other day, and said he wanted to sell his outfit. So I bought him out. He was pining to get back to Brooklyn and write a book."

"That book o' his!" said Mrs. Pratt. "He was always talkin' on it, but I don't believe he ever started it yet."

"Whereabout do you come from, Miss McGill?" said Pratt. I could see he was mighty puzzled at a woman driving a vanload of books around the country, alone.

"Over toward Redfield," I said.

"You any kin to that writer that lives up that way?"

"You mean Andrew McGill?" I said. "He's my brother."

"Do tell!" exclaimed Mrs. Pratt. "Why the Perfessor thought a terrible lot of him. He read us all to sleep with one of his books one night. Said he was the best literature in this State, I do believe."

I smiled to myself as I thought of the set-to on the road   from Shelby.

"Well," said Pratt, "if the Perfessor's got any better friends than us in these parts, I'm glad to meet 'em. He come here first time 'bout four years ago. I was up working in the hayfield that afternoon, and I heard a shout down by the mill pond. I looked over that way and saw a couple o' kids waving their arms and screamin'. I ran down the hill and there was the Perfessor just a pullin' my boy Dick out o' the water. Dick's this one over here."

Dick, a small boy of thirteen or so, grew red under his freckles.

"The kids had been foolin' around on a raft there, an' first thing you know Dick fell in, right into deep water, over by the dam. Couldn't swim a stroke, neither. And the Perfessor, who jest happened to be comin' along in that 'bus of his, heard the boys yell. Didn't he hop out o' the wagon as spry as a chimpanzee, skin over the fence, an' jump into the pond, swim out there an' tow the boy in! Yes, ma'am, he saved that boy's life then an' no mistake. That man can read me to sleep with poetry any night he has a mind to. He's a plumb fine little firecracker, the Perfessor."

Farmer Pratt pulled hard on his pipe. Evidently his friendship for the wandering bookseller was one of the realities of his life.

"Yes, ma'am," he went on, "that Perfessor has been a good friend to me, sure enough. We brought him an' the boy back to the house. The boy had gone down three times an' the Perfessor had to dive to find him. They were both purty well all in, an' I tell you I was scared. But we got Dick around somehow—rolled him on a sugar bar'l, an' poured whiskey in him, an' worked his arms, an' put him in hot blankets. By and by he come to. An' then I found that the Perfessor, gettin' over the barbwire fence so quick (when he lit for the pond) had torn a hole in his leg you could put four fingers in. There was his trouser all stiff with blood, an' he not sayin' a thing. Pluckiest little runt in three States, by Judas! Well, we put *him* to bed, too, and then the Missus keeled over, an' we put *her* to bed. Three of them, by time the Doc got here. Great old summer afternoon that was! But bless your heart, we couldn't keep the Perfessor abed long.

Next day he was out lookin' fer his poetry books, an' first thing you know he had us all rounded up an' was preachin' good literature at us like any evangelist. I guess we all fell asleep over his poetry, so then he started on readin' that 'Treasure Island' story to us, wasn't it, Mother? By hickory, we none of us fell asleep over that. He started the kids readin' so they been at it ever since, and Dick's top boy at school now. Teacher says she never saw such a boy for readin'. That's what Perfessor done for us! Well, tell us 'bout yerself, Miss McGill. Is there any good books we ought to read? I used to pine for some o' that feller Shakespeare my father used to talk about so much, but Perfessor always 'lowed it was over my head!"

It gave me quite a thrill to hear all this about Mifflin. I could readily imagine the masterful little man captivating the simple-hearted Pratts with his eloquence and earnestness. And the story of the mill pond had its meaning, too. Little Redbeard was no mere wandering crank—he was a real man, cool and steady of brain, with the earmarks of a hero. I felt a sudden gush of warmth as I recalled his comical ways.

Mrs. Pratt lit a fire in her Franklin stove and I racked my head wondering how I could tread worthily in the Professor's footsteps. Finally I fetched the "Jungle Book" from Parnassus and read them the story of Rikki-Tikki-Tavi. There was a long pause when I had finished.

"Say, Pa," said Dick shyly, "that mongoose was rather like

Professor, wasn't he!"

Plainly the Professor was the traditional hero of this family, and I began to feel rather like an impostor!

I suppose it was foolish of me, but I had already made up my mind to push on to Woodbridge that night. It could not be more than four miles, and the time was not much after eight. I felt a little twinge of quite unworthy annoyance because I was still treading in the glamour of the Professor's influence. The Pratts would talk of nothing else, and I wanted to get somewhere where I would be estimated at my own value, not merely as his disciple. "Darn the Redbeard," I said to myself, "I think he has bewitched these people!" And in spite of their protests and invitations to stay the night, I insisted on having Peg hitched up. I gave them the copy of the "Jungle Book" as a small return for their hospitality, and finally sold Mr. Pratt a little copy of "Lamb's Tales from Shakespeare" which I thought he could read without brain fever. Then I lit my lantern and after a chorus of good-byes Parnassus rolled away. "Well," I said to myself as I turned into the high road once more, "drat the gingersnap, he seems to hypnotize everybody... he must be nearly in Brooklyn by this time!"

It was very quiet along the road, also very dark, for the sky had clouded over and I could see neither moon nor stars. As it was a direct road I should have had no difficulty, and I suppose I must have fallen into a doze during which Peg took a wrong turning. At any rate, I realized about half-past nine that Parnassus was on a much rougher road than the highway had any right to be, and there were no telephone poles to be seen. I knew that they stretched all along the main road, so plainly I had made a mistake. I was reluctant for a moment to admit that I could be wrong, and just then Peg stumbled heavily and stood still. She paid no heed to my exhortations, and when I got out and carried my lantern to see whether anything was in the way, I found that she had cast a shoe and her foot was bleeding. The shoe must have dropped off some way back and she had picked up a nail or something in the quick. I saw no alternative but to stay where I was for the night.

This was not very pleasant, but the adventures of the day had put me into a stoical frame of mind, and I saw no good in repining. I unhitched Peg, sponged her foot, and tied her to a tree. I would have made more careful explorations to determine just where I was, but a sharp patter of rain began to fall. So I climbed into my Parnassus, took Bock in with me, and lit the swinging lamp. By this time it was nearly ten o'clock. There was nothing to do but turn in, so I took off my boots and lay down in the bunk. Bock lay quite comfortably on the floor of the van. I meant to read for a while, and so did not turn out the light, but I fell asleep almost immediately.

I woke up at half-past eleven and turned out the lamp, which had made the van very warm. I opened the little windows front and back, and would have opened the door, but I feared Bock might slip away. It was still raining a little. To my annoyance I felt very wakeful. I lay for some time listening to the patter of raindrops on the roof and skylight—a very snug sound when one is warm and safe. Every now and then I could hear Peg stamping in the underbrush. I was almost dozing off again when Bock gave a low growl.

No woman of my bulk has a right to be nervous, I guess, but instantly my security vanished! The patter of the rain seemed menacing, and I imagined a hundred horrors. I was totally alone and unarmed, and Bock was not a large dog. He growled again, and I felt worse than before. I imagined that I heard stealthy sounds in the bushes, and once Peg snorted as though frightened. I put my hand down to pat Bock, and found that his neck was all bristly, like a fighting cock. He uttered a queer half growl, half whine, which gave me a chill. Some one must be prowling about the van, but in the falling rain I could hear nothing.

I felt I must do something. I was afraid to call out lest I betray the fact that there was only a woman in the van. My expedient was absurd enough, but at any rate it satisfied my desire to act. I seized one of my boots and banged vigorously on the floor, at the same time growling in as deep and masculine a voice as I could muster: "What the hell's the matter? What the hell's the matter?" This sounds silly enough, I dare say, but it afforded me some relief. And as Bock shortly ceased growling, it apparently served some purpose.

I lay awake for a long time, tingling all over with nervousness. Then I began to grow calmer, and was getting drowsy almost in spite of myself when I was aroused by the unmistakable sound of Bock's tail thumping on the floor—a sure sign of pleasure. This puzzled me quite as much as his growls. I did not dare strike a light, but could hear him sniffing at the door of the van and whining with eagerness. This seemed very uncanny, and again I crept stealthily out of the bunk and pounded on the floor lustily, this time with the frying pan, which made an unearthly din. Peg neighed and snorted, and Bock began to bark. Even in my anxiety I almost laughed. "It sounds like an insane asylum," I thought, and reflected that probably the disturbance was only caused by some small animal. Perhaps a rabbit or a skunk which Bock had winded and wanted to chase. I patted him, and crawled into my bunk once more.

But my real excitement was still to come. About half an hour later I heard unmistakable footsteps alongside the van. Bock growled furiously, and I lay in a panic. Something jarred one of the wheels. Then broke out a most extraordinary racket. I heard quick steps, Peg whinneyed, and something fell heavily against the back of the wagon. There was a violent scuffle on the ground, the sound of blows, and rapid breathing. With my heart jumping I peered out of one of the back windows. There was barely any light, but dimly I could see a tumbling mass which squirmed and writhed on the ground. Something struck one of the rear wheels so that

Parnassus trembled. I heard hoarse swearing, and then the whole body, whatever it was, rolled off into the underbrush. There was a terrific crashing and snapping of twigs. Bock whined, growled, and pawed madly at the door. And then complete silence.

My nerves were quite shattered by this time. I don't think I had been so frightened since childhood days when I awakened from a nightmare. Little trickles of fear crept up and down my spine and my scalp prickled. I pulled Bock on the bunk, and lay with one hand on his collar. He, too, seemed agitated and sniffed gingerly now and then. Finally, however, he gave a sigh and fell asleep. I judged it might have been two o'clock, but I did not like to strike a light. And at last I fell into a doze.

When I woke the sun was shining brilliantly and the air was full of the chirping of birds. I felt stiff and uneasy from sleeping in my clothes, and my foot was numb from Bock's weight.

I got up and looked out of the window. Parnassus was standing in a narrow lane by a grove of birch trees. The ground was muddy, and smeared with footprints behind the van. I opened the door and looked around. The first thing I saw, on the ground by one of the wheels, was a battered   tweed   cap.

Chapter 9

My feelings were as mixed as a crushed nut sundae. So the Professor hadn't gone to Brooklyn after all! What did he mean by prowling after me like a sleuth? Was it just homesickness for Parnassus? Not likely! And then the horrible noises I had heard in the night; had some tramp been hanging about the van in the hope of robbing me? Had the tramp attacked Mifflin? Or had Mifflin attacked the tramp? Who had got the better of it?

I picked up the muddy cap and threw it into the van. Anyway, I had problems of my own to tackle, and those of the Professor could wait.

Peg whinneyed when she saw me. I examined her foot. Seeing it by daylight the trouble was not hard to diagnose. A long, jagged piece of slate was wedged in the frog of the foot. I easily wrenched it out, heated some water, and gave the hoof another sponging. It would be all right when shod once more. But where was the shoe?

I gave the horse some oats, cooked an egg and a cup of coffee for myself at the little kerosene stove, and broke up a dog biscuit for Bock. I marvelled once more at the completeness of Parnassus' furnishings. Bock helped me to scour the pan. He sniffed eagerly at the cap when I showed it to him, and wagged his tail.

It seemed to me that the only thing I could do was to leave Parnassus and the animals where they were and retrace my steps as far as the Pratt farm. Undoubtedly Mr. Pratt would be glad to sell me a horse-shoe and send his hired man to do the job for me. I could not drive Peg as she was, with a sore foot and without a shoe. I judged Parnassus would be quite safe: the lane seemed to be a lonely one leading to a deserted quarry. I tied Bock to the steps to act as a guard, took my purse and the Professor's cap with me, locked the door of the van, and set off along the back track. Bock whined and tugged violently when he saw me disappearing, but I could see no other course.

The lane rejoined the main road about half a mile back. I must have been asleep or I could never have made the mistake of turning off. I don't see why Peg should have made the turn, unless her foot hurt and she judged the side track would be a good place to rest. She must have been well used to stopping overnight in the open.

I strode along pondering over my adventures, and resolved to buy a pistol when I got to Woodbridge. I remember thinking that I could write quite a book now myself. Already I began to feel quite a hardened pioneer. It doesn't take an adaptable person long to accustom one's self to a new way of life, and the humdrum routine of the farm certainly looked prosy compared to voyaging with Parnassus. When I had got beyond Woodbridge, and had crossed the river, I would begin to sell books in earnest. Also I would buy a notebook and jot down my experiences. I had heard of bookselling as a profession for women, but I thought that my taste of it was probably unique. I might even write a book that would rival Andrew's—yes, and Mifflin's. And that brought my thoughts to Barbarossa again.

Of all extraordinary people, I thought, he certainly takes the cake—and then, rounding a bend, I saw him sitting on a rail fence, with his head shining in the sunlight. My heart gave a sort of jump. I do believe I was getting fond of the Professor. He was examining something which he held in his hand.

"You'll get sunstroke," I said. "Here's your cap." And I pulled it out of my pocket and tossed it to him.

"Thanks," he said, as cool as you please. "And here's your horse-shoe. Fair exchange!"

I burst out laughing, and he looked disconcerted, as I hoped he would.

"I thought you'd be in Brooklyn by now," I said, "at 600 Abingdon Avenue, laying out Chapter One. What do you mean by following me this way? You nearly frightened me to death last night. I felt like one of Fenimore Cooper's heroines, shut up in the blockhouse while the redskins prowled about."

He flushed and looked very uncomfortable.

"I owe you an apology," he said. "I certainly never intended that you should see me. I bought a ticket for New York and checked my bag through. And then while I was waiting for the train it came over me that your brother was right, and that it was a darned risky thing for you to go jaunting about alone in Parnassus. I was afraid something might happen. I followed along the road behind you, keeping well out of sight."

"Where were you while I was at Pratt's?"

"Sitting not far down the road eating bread and cheese," he said. "Also I wrote a poem, a thing I very rarely do."

"Well, I hope your ears burned," I said, "for those Pratts have certainly raised you to the peerage."

He got more uncomfortable than ever.

"Well," he said, "I dare say it was all an error, but anyway I *did* follow you. When you turned off into that lane, I kept pretty close behind you. As it happens, I know this bit of country, and there are very often some hoboes hanging around the old quarry up that lane. They have a cave there where they go into winter quarters. I was afraid some of them might bother you. You could hardly have chosen a worse place to camp out. By the bones of George Eliot, Pratt ought to have warned you. I can't conceive why you didn't stop at his house overnight anyway."

"If you must know, I got weary of hearing them sing your praises."

I could see that he was beginning to get nettled.

"I regret having alarmed you," he said. "I see that Peg has dropped a shoe. If you'll let me fix it for you, after that I won't bother you."

We turned back again along the road, and I noticed the right side of his face for the first time. Under the ear was a large livid bruise.

"That hobo, or whoever he was," I said, "must have been a better fighter than Andrew. I see he landed on your cheek. Are you always fighting?"

His annoyance disappeared. Apparently the Professor enjoyed a fight almost as much as he did a good book.

"Please don't regard the last twenty-four hours as typical of me," he said with a chuckle. "I am so unused to being a squire of dames that perhaps I take the responsibilities too seriously."

"Did you sleep at all last night?" I asked. I think I began to realize for the first time that the gallant little creature had been out all night in a drizzling rain, simply to guard me from possible annoyance; and I had been unforgivably churlish about it.

"I found a very fine haystack in a field overlooking the quarry. I crawled into the middle of it. A haystack is sometimes more comfortable than a boarding-house."

"Well," I said penitently, "I can never forgive myself for the trouble I've caused you. It was awfully good of you to do what you did. Please put your cap on and don't catch cold."

We walked for several minutes in silence. I watched him out of the corner of my eye. I was afraid he might have caught his death of cold from being out all night in the wet, to say nothing of the scuffle he had had with the tramp; but he really looked as chipper as ever.

"How do you like the wild life of a bookseller?" he said.

"You must read George Borrow. He would have enjoyed Parnassus."

"I was just thinking, when I met you, that I could write a book about my adventures."

"Good!" he said. "We might collaborate."

"There's another thing we might collaborate on," I said, "and that's breakfast. I'm sure you haven't had any."

"No," he said, "I don't think I have. I never lie when I know
I shan't be believed."

"I haven't had any, either," I said. I thought that to tell an untruth would be the least thing I could do to reward the little man for his unselfishness.

"Well," he said, "I really thought that by this time—"

He broke off. "Was that Bock barking?" he asked sharply.

We had been walking slowly, and had not yet reached the spot where the lane branched from the main road. We were still about three quarters of a mile from the place where I had camped overnight. We both listened carefully, but I could hear nothing but the singing of the telephone wires along the road.

"No matter," he said. "I thought I heard a dog." But I noticed that he quickened his pace.

"I was saying," he continued, "that I had really thought to have lost Parnassus for good by this morning, but I'm tickled to death to have a chance to see her again. I hope she'll be as good a friend to you as she has

78

been to me. I suppose you'll sell her when you return to the Sage?"

"I don't know I'm sure," I said. "I must confess I'm still a little at sea. My desire for an adventure seems to have let me in deeper than I expected. I begin to see that there's more in this bookselling game than I thought. Honestly, it's getting into my blood."

"Well, that's fine," he said heartily. "I couldn't have left Parnassus in better hands. You must let me know what you do with her, and then perhaps, when I've finished my book, I can buy her back."

We struck off into the lane. The ground was slippery under the trees and we went single file, Mifflin in front. I looked at my watch—it was nine o'clock, just an hour since I had left the van. As we neared the spot Mifflin kept looking ahead through the birch trees in a queer way.

"What's the matter?" I said. "We're almost there, aren't we?"

"We *are* there," he said. "Here's the place."

Parnassus   was   gone!

Chapter 10

We stood in complete dismay—I did, at any rate—for about as long as it takes to peel a potato. There could be no doubt in which direction the van had moved, for the track of the wheels was plain. It had gone farther up the lane toward the quarry. In the earth, which was still soggy, were a number of footprints.

"By the bones of Polycarp!" exclaimed the Professor, "those hoboes have stolen the van. I guess they think it'll make a fine Pullman sleeper for them. If I'd realized there was more than one of them I'd have hung around closer. They need a lesson."

Good Lord! I thought, here's Don Quixote about to wade into another fight.

"Hadn't we better go back and get Mr. Pratt?" I asked.

This was obviously the wrong thing to say. It put the fiery little man all the more on his mettle. His beard bristled. "Nothing of the sort!" he said. "Those fellows are cowards and vagabonds anyway. They can't be far off; you haven't been away more than an hour, have you? If they've done anything to Bock, by the bones of Chaucer, I'll harry them. I *thought* I heard him bark."

He hurried up the lane, and I followed in a panicky frame of mind. The track wound along a hillside, between a high bank and a forest of birch trees. I think the distance can't have been more than a quarter of a mile. Anyway, in a very few minutes the road made a sharp twist to the right and we found ourselves looking down into the quarry, over a sheer rocky drop of a hundred feet at least. Below, drawn over to one side of the wall of rock, stood Parnassus. Peg was between the shafts. Bock was nowhere to be seen. Sitting by the van were three disreputable looking men. The smoke of a cooking fire rose into the air; evidently they were making free with my little larder.

"Keep back," said the Professor softly. "Don't let them see us." He flattened himself in the grass and crawled to the edge of the cliff. I did the same, and we lay there, invisible from below, but quite able to see everything in the quarry. The three tramps were evidently enjoying an excellent breakfast.

"This place is a regular hang-out for these fellows," Mifflin whispered. "I've seen hoboes about here every year. They go into winter quarters about the end of October, usually. There's an old blasted-out section of this quarry that makes a sheltered dormitory for them, and as the place isn't worked any more they're not disturbed here so long as they don't make mischief in the neighbourhood. We'll give them...."

"Hands up!" said a rough voice behind us. I looked round. There was a fat, red-faced villainous-looking creature covering us with a shiny revolver. It was an awkward situation. Both the Professor and I were lying full length on the ground. We were quite helpless.

"Get up!" said the tramp in a husky, nasty voice. "I guess youse thought we wasn't covering our trail? Well, we'll have to tie you up, I reckon, while we get away with this Crystal Pallis of yourn."

I scrambled to my feet, but to my surprise the Professor continued to lie at full length.

"Get up, deacon!" said the tramp again. "Get up on them graceful limbs, *if* you please."

I guess he thought himself safe from attack by a woman. At any rate, he bent over as if to grab Mifflin by the neck. I saw my chance and jumped on him from

81

behind. I am heavy, as I have said, and he sprawled on the ground. My doubts as to the pistol being loaded were promptly dissolved, for it went off like a cannon. Nobody was in front of it, however, and Mifflin was on his feet like a flash. He had the ruffian by the throat and kicked the weapon out of his hand. I ran to seize it.

"You son of Satan!" said the valiant Redbeard. "Thought you could bully us, did you? Miss McGill, you were as quick as Joan of Arc. Hand me the pistol, please."

I gave it to him, and he shoved it under the hobo's nose.

"Now," he said, "take off that rag around your neck."

The rag was an old red handkerchief, inconceivably soiled. The tramp removed it, grumbling and whining. Mifflin gave me the pistol to hold while he tied our prisoner's wrists together. In the meantime we heard a shout from the quarry. The three vagabonds were gazing up in great excitement.

"You tell those fashion plates down there," said Mifflin, as he knotted the tramp's hands together, "that if they make any fight I'll shoot them like crows." His voice was cold and savage and he seemed quite master of the situation, but I must confess I wondered how we could handle four of them.

The greasy ruffian shouted down to his pals in the quarry, but I did not hear what he said, as just then the Professor asked me to keep our captive covered while he got a stick. I stood with the pistol pointed at his head while Mifflin ran back into the birchwood to cut a cudgel.

The tramp's face became the colour of the under side of a fried egg as he looked into the muzzle of his own gun.

"Say, lady," he pleaded, "that gun goes off awful easy, point her somewhere else or you'll croak me by mistake."

I thought a good scare wouldn't do him any harm and kept the barrel steadily on him.

The rascals down below seemed debating what to do. I don't know whether they were armed or not; but probably they imagined that there were more than two of us. At all events, by the time Mifflin came back with a stout birch staff they were hustling out of the quarry on the lower side. The Professor swore, and looked as if he would gladly give chase, but he refrained.

"Here, you," he said in crisp tones to the tramp, "march on ahead of us, down to the quarry."

The fat ruffian shambled awkwardly down the trail. We had to make quite a detour to get into the quarry, and by the time we reached there the other three tramps had got clean away. I was not sorry, to tell the truth. I thought the Professor had had enough scrapping for one twenty-four hours.

Peg whinneyed loudly as she saw us coming, but Bock was not in sight.

"What have you done with the dog, you swine?" said Mifflin. "If you've hurt him I'll make you pay with your own hide."

Our prisoner was completely cowed. "No, boss, we ain't hurt the dog," he fawned. "We tied him up so he couldn't bark, that's all. He's in the 'bus." And sure enough, by this time we could hear smothered yelping and whining from Parnassus.

I hurried to open the door, and there was Bock, his jaws tied together with a rope-end. He bounded out and made super-canine efforts to express his joy at seeing the Professor again. He paid very little attention to me.

"Well," said Mifflin, after freeing the dog's muzzle, and with difficulty restraining him from burying his teeth in the tramp's shin, "what shall we do with this heroic specimen of manhood? Shall we cart him over to the jail in Port Vigor, or shall we let him go?"

The tramp burst into a whining appeal that was almost funny, it was so abject. The Professor cut it short.

"I ought to pack you into quod," he said. "Are you the Phoebus Apollo I scuffled with down the lane last night? Was it you skulking around this wagon then?"

"No, boss, that was Splitlip Sam, honest to Gawd it was. He come back, boss; said he'd been fightin' with a cat-o'-mountain! Say, boss, you sure hit him hard. One of his lamps is a pudding! Boss, I'll swear I ain't had nothin' to do with it."

"I don't like your society," said the Professor, "and I'm going to turn you loose. I'm going to count ten, and if you're not out of this quarry by then, I'll shoot. And if I see you again I'll skin you alive. Now get out!"

He cut the knotted handkerchief in two. The hobo needed no urging. He spun on his heel and fled like a rabbit. The Professor watched him go, and as the fat, ungainly figure burst through a hedge and disappeared he fired the revolver into the air to frighten him still more. Then he tossed the weapon into the pool near by.

"Well, Miss McGill," he said with a chuckle, "if you like to undertake breakfast, I'll fix up Peg." And he drew the horse-shoe from his pocket once more.

A brief inspection of Parnassus satisfied me that the thieves had not had time to do any real damage. They had got out most of the eatables and spread them on a flat rock in preparation for a feast; and they had tracked a good deal of mud into the van; but otherwise I could see nothing amiss. So while Mifflin busied himself with Peg's foot it was easy for me to get a meal under way. I found a gush of clean water trickling down the face of the rock. There were still some eggs and bread and cheese in the little cupboard, and an unopened tin of condensed milk. I gave Peg her nose bag of oats, and fed Bock, who was frisking about in high spirits. By that time the shoeing was done, and the Professor and I sat down to an improvised meal. I was beginning to feel as if this gipsy existence were the normal course of my life.

"Well, Professor," I said, as I handed him a cup of coffee and a plate of scrambled eggs and cheese, "for a man who slept in a wet haystack, you acquit yourself with excellent valour."

"Old Parnassus is quite a stormy petrel," he said. "I used to think the chief difficulty in writing a book would be to invent things to happen, but if I were to sit down and write the adventures I'd had with her it would be a regular Odyssey."

"How about Peg's foot?" I asked. "Can she travel on it?"

"It'll be all right if you go easy. I've scraped out the injured part and put the shoe back. I keep a little kit of tools under the van for emergencies of all sorts."

It was chilly, and we didn't dawdle over our meal. I only made a feint of eating, as I had had a little breakfast before, and also as the events of the last few hours had left me rather restless. I wanted to get Parnassus out on the highway again, to jog along in the sun and think things over. The quarry was a desolate, forbidding place anyway. But before we left we explored the cave where the tramps had been preparing to make themselves comfortable for the winter. It was not really a cave, but only a shaft into the granite cliff. A screen of evergreen boughs protected the opening against the weather, and inside were piles of sacking that had evidently been used as beds, and many old grocery boxes for tables and chairs. It amused me to notice a cracked fragment of mirror balanced on a corner of rock. Even these ragamuffins apparently were not totally unconscious of personal appearance. I seized the opportunity, while the Professor was giving Peg's foot a final look, to rearrange my hair, which was emphatically a sight. I hardly think Andrew would have recognized me that morning.

We led Peg up the steep incline, back into the lane where I had strayed, and at length we reached the main road again. Here I began to lay down the law to Redbeard.

"Now look here, Professor," I said, "I'm not going to have you tramp all the way back to Port Vigor. After the night you've had you need a rest. You just climb into that Parnassus and lie down for a good snooze. I'll drive you into Woodbridge and you can take your train there. Now you get right into that bunk. I'll sit out here and drive."

He demurred, but without much emphasis. I think the little fool was just about fagged out, and no wonder. I was a trifle groggy myself. In the end he was quite docile. He climbed into the van, took off his boots, and lay down under a blanket. Bock followed him, and I think they both fell asleep on the instant. I got on the front seat and took the reins. I didn't let Peg go more quickly than a walk as I wanted to spare her sore foot.

My, what a morning that was after the rain! The road ran pretty close to the shore, and every now and then I could catch a glimpse of the water. The air was keen— not just the ordinary, unnoticed air that we breathe in and out and don't think about, but a sharp and tingling essence, as strong in the nostrils as camphor or ammonia. The sun seemed focussed upon Parnassus, and we moved along the white road in a flush of golden light. The flat fronds of the cedars swayed gently in the salty air, and for the first time in ten years, I should think, I began amusing myself by selecting words to describe the goodness of the morning. I even imagined myself writing a description of it, as if I were Andrew or Thoreau. The crazy little Professor had inoculated me with his literary bug, I guess.

And then I did a dishonourable thing. Just by chance I put my hand into the little pocket beside the seat where Mifflin kept a few odds and ends. I meant to have another look at that card of his with the poem on it. And there I found a funny, battered little notebook, evidently forgotten. On the cover was written, in ink, "Thoughts on the Present Discontents." That title seemed vaguely familiar. I seemed to recall something of the kind from my school days—more than twenty years ago, goodness me! Of course if I had been honourable I wouldn't have looked into it. But in a kind of quibbling self-justification I recalled that I had bought Parnassus and all it contained, "lock, stock, barrel and bung" as Andrew used to say. And so....

The notebook was full of little jottings, written in pencil in the Professor's small, precise hand. The words were rubbed and soiled, but plainly legible. I read this:

I don't suppose Bock or Peg get lonely, but by the bones of Ben Gunn, I do. Seems silly when Herrick and Hans Andersen and Tennyson and Thoreau and a whole wagonload of other good fellows are riding at my back. I can hear them all talking as we trundle along. But books aren't a *substantial* world after all, and every now and then we get hungry for some closer, more human relationships. I've been totally alone now for eight years—except for Runt, and he might be dead and never say so. This wandering about is fine in its way, but it must come to an end some day. A man needs to put down a root somewhere to be really happy.

What absurd victims of contrary desires we are! If a man is settled in one place he yearns to wander; when he wanders he yearns to have a home. And yet how bestial is content—all the great things in life are done by discontented people.

There are three ingredients in the good life: learning, earning, and yearning. A man should be learning as he goes; and he should be earning bread for himself and others; and he should be yearning, too: yearning to know the unknowable.

What a fine old poem is "The Pulley" by George Herbert! Those Elizabethan fellows knew how to write! They were marred perhaps by their idea that poems must be "witty." (Remember how Bacon said that reading poets makes one witty? There he gave a clue to the literature of his time.) Their fantastic puns and conceits are rather out of our fashion nowadays. But Lord! the root of the matter was in them! How gallantly, how reverently, they tackle the problems of life!

When God at first made man (says George Herbert) He had a "glass of blessings standing by." So He pours on man all the blessings in His reservoir: strength, beauty, wisdom, honour, pleasure—and then He refrains from giving him the last of them, which is rest, i.e., contentment. God sees that if man is contented he will never win his way to Him. Let man be restless, so that

> "If goodness lead him not, yet weariness
> May toss him to My breast."

Some day I shall write a novel on that theme, and call it "The Pulley." In this tragic, restless world there must be some place where at last we can lay our heads and be at rest. Some people call it death. Some call it God.

My ideal of a man is not the Omar who wants to shatter into bits this sorry scheme of things, and then remould it nearer to the heart's desire. Old Omar was a coward, with his silk pajamas and his glass of wine. The real man is George Herbert's "seasoned timber"—the fellow who does handily and well whatever comes to him. Even if it's only shovelling coal into a furnace he can balance the shovel neatly, swing the coal square on the fire and not spill it on the floor. If it's only splitting kindling or running a trolley car he can make a good, artistic job of it. If it's only writing a book or peeling potatoes he can put into it the best he has. Even if he's only a bald-headed old fool over forty selling books on a country road, he can make an ideal of it. Good old Parnassus! It's a great game.... I think I'll have to give her up soon, though: I must get that book of mine written. But Parnassus has been a true glass of blessings to me.

There was much more in the notebook; indeed it was half full of jotted paragraphs, memoranda, and scraps of writing—poems I believe some of them were—but I had seen enough. It seemed as if I had stumbled unawares on the pathetic, brave, and lonely heart of the little man. I'm a commonplace creature, I'm afraid, insensible to many of the deeper things in life, but every now and then, like all of us, I come face to face with something that thrills me. I saw how this little, red-bearded pedlar was like a cake of yeast in the big, heavy dough of humanity: how he travelled about trying to fulfil in his own way his ideals of beauty. I felt almost motherly toward him: I wanted to tell him that I understood him. And in a way I felt ashamed of having run away from my own homely tasks, my kitchen and my hen yard and dear old, hot-tempered, absent-minded Andrew. I fell into a sober mood. As soon as I was alone, I thought, I would sell Parnassus and hurry back to the farm. That was my job, that was my glass of blessings. What was I doing—a fat, middle-aged woman—trapesing along the roads with a cartload of books I didn't understand?

I slipped the little notebook back into its hiding-place. I would have died rather than let the Professor know I had seen it.

Chapter 11

We were coming into Woodbridge; and I was just wondering whether to wake the Professor when the little window behind me slid back and he stuck his head out.

"Hello!" he said. "I think I must have been asleep!"

"Well, I should hope so," I said. "You needed it."

Indeed he looked much better, and I was relieved to see it. I had been really afraid he would be ill after sleeping out all night, but I guess he was tougher than I thought. He joined me on the seat, and we drove into the town. While he went to the station to ask about the trains I had a fine time selling books. I was away from the locality where I was known, and had no shyness in attempting to imitate Mifflin's methods. I even went him one better by going into a hardware store where I bought a large dinner bell. This I rang lustily until a crowd gathered, then I put up the flaps and displayed my books. As a matter of fact, I sold only one, but I enjoyed myself none the less.

By and by Mifflin reappeared. I think he had been to a barber: at any rate he looked very spry: he had bought a clean collar and a flowing tie of a bright electric blue which really suited him rather well.

"Well," he said, "the Sage is going to get back at me for that punch on the nose! I've been to the bank to cash your check. They telephoned over to Redfield, and apparently your brother has stopped payment on it. It's rather awkward: they seem to think I'm a crook."

I was furious. What right had Andrew to do that?

"The brute!" I said. "What on earth shall I do?"

"I suggest that you telephone to the Redfield Bank," he said, "and countermand your brother's instructions— that is, unless you think you've made a mistake? I don't want to take advantage of you."

"Nonsense!" I said. "I'm not going to let Andrew spoil my holiday. That's always his way: if he gets an idea into his head he's like a mule. I'll telephone to Redfield, and then we'll go to see the bank here."

We put Parnassus up at the hotel, and I went to the telephone. I was thoroughly angry at Andrew, and tried to get him on the wire first. But Sabine Farm didn't answer. Then I telephoned to the bank in Redfield, and got Mr. Shirley. He's the cashier, and I know him well. I guess he recognized my voice, for he made no objection when I told him what I wanted.

"Now you telephone to the bank in Woodbridge," I said, "and tell them to let Mr. Mifflin have the money. I'll go there with him to identify him. Will that be all right?"

"Perfectly," he said. The deceitful little snail! If I had only known what he was concocting!

Mifflin said there was a train at three o'clock which he could take. We stopped at a little lunch room for a bite to eat, then he went again to the bank, and I with him. We asked the cashier whether they had had a message from Redfield.

"Yes," he said. "We've just heard." And he looked at me rather queerly.

"Are you Miss McGill?" he said.

"I am," I said.

"Will you just step this way a moment?" he asked politely.

He led me into a little sitting-room and asked me to sit down. I supposed that he was going to get some paper for me to sign, so I waited quite patiently for several minutes. I had left the Professor at the cashier's window, where they would give him his money.

I waited some time, and finally I got tired of looking at the Life Insurance calendars. Then I happened to glance out of the window. Surely that was the Professor, just disappearing round the corner with another man?

I returned to the cashier's desk.

"What's the matter?" I said. "Your mahogany furniture is charming, but I'm tired of it. Do I have to sit here any longer? And where's Mr. Mifflin? Did he get his money?"

The cashier was a horrid little creature with side whiskers.

"I'm sorry you had to wait, Madam," he said. "The transaction is just concluded. We gave Mr. Mifflin what was due him. There is no need for you to stay longer."

I thought this was very extraordinary. Surely the Professor would not leave without saying good-bye? However, I noticed that the clock said three minutes to three, so I thought that perhaps he had had to run to catch his train. He was such a strange little man, anyway....

Well, I went back to the hotel, quite a little upset by this sudden parting. At least I was glad the little man had got his money all right. Probably he would write from Brooklyn, but of course I wouldn't get the letter till I returned to the farm as that was the only address he would have. Perhaps that wouldn't be so long after all: but I did not feel like going back now, when Andrew had been so horrid.

I drove Parnassus on the ferry, and we crossed the river. I felt lost and disagreeable. Even the fresh movement through the air gave me no pleasure. Bock whined dismally inside the van.

It didn't take me long to discover that Parnassing all alone had lost some of its charms. I missed the Professor: missed his abrupt, direct way of saying things, and his whimsical wit. And I was annoyed by his skipping off without a word of good-bye. It didn't seem natural. I partially appeased my irritation by stopping at a farmhouse on the other side of the river and selling a cook book. Then I started along the road for Bath—about five miles farther on. Peg's foot didn't seem to bother her so I thought it would be safe to travel that far before stopping for the night. Counting up the days (with some difficulty: it seemed as though I had been away from home a month), I remembered that this was Saturday night. I thought I would stay in Bath over Sunday and get a good rest. We jogged sedately along the road, and I got out a copy of "Vanity Fair." I was so absorbed in Becky Sharp that I wouldn't even interrupt myself to sell books at the houses we passed. I think reading a good book makes one modest. When you see the marvellous insight into human nature which a truly great book shows, it is bound to make you feel small—like looking at the Dipper on a clear night, or seeing the winter sunrise when you go out to collect the morning eggs. And anything that makes you feel small is mighty good for you.

"What do you mean by a great book?" said the Professor—I mean, I imagined him saying it. It seemed to me as if I could see him sitting there, with his corncob pipe in his hand and that quizzical little face of his looking sharply at me. Somehow, talking with the Professor had made me think. He was as good as one of those Scranton correspondence courses, I do believe, and no money to pay for postage.

Well, I said to the Professor—to myself I mean—let's see: what *is* a good book? I don't mean books like Henry James's (he's Andrew's great idol. It always seemed to me that he had a kind of rush of words to the head and never stopped to sort them out properly). A good book ought to have something simple about it. And, like Eve, it ought to come from somewhere near the third rib: there ought to be a heart beating in it. A story that's all forehead doesn't amount to much. Anyway, it'll never get over at a Dorcas meeting. That was the trouble with Henry James. Andrew talked so much about him that I took one of his books to read aloud at our sewing circle over at Redfield. Well, after one try we had to fall back on "Pollyanna."

I haven't been doing chores and running a farmhouse for fifteen years without getting some ideas about life—and even about books. I wouldn't set my lit'ry views up against yours, Professor (I was still talking to Mifflin in my mind), no, nor even against Andrew's—but as I say, I've got some ideas of my own. I've learned that honest work counts in writing books just as much as it does in washing dishes. I guess Andrew's books must be some good after all because he surely does mull over them without end. I can forgive his being a shiftless farmer so long as he really does his literary chores up to the hilt. A man can be slack in everything else, if he does one thing as well as he possibly can. And I guess it won't matter my being an ignoramus in literature so long as I'm rated A-1 in the kitchen. That's what I used to think as I polished and scoured and scrubbed and dusted and swept and then set about getting dinner. If I ever sat down to read for ten minutes the cat would get into the custard. No woman in the country sits down for fifteen consecutive minutes between sunrise and sunset, anyway, unless she has half a dozen servants. And nobody knows anything about literature unless he spends most of his life sitting down. So there you are.

The cultivation of philosophic reflection was a new experience for me. Peg ambled along contentedly and the dog trailed under Parnassus where I had tied him. I read "Vanity Fair" and thought about all sorts of things. Once I got out to pick some scarlet maple leaves that attracted me. The motors passing annoyed me with their dust and noise, but by and by one of them stopped, looked at my outfit curiously, and then asked to see some books. I put up the flaps for them and we pulled off to one side of the road and had a good talk. They bought two or three books, too.

By the time I neared Bath the hands of my watch pointed to supper. I was still a bit shy of Mifflin's scheme of stopping overnight at farmhouses, so I thought I'd go right into the town and look for a hotel. The next day was Sunday, so it seemed reasonable to give the horse a good rest and stay in Bath two nights. The Hominy House looked clean and old-fashioned, and the name amused me, so in I went. It was a kind of high-class boarding-house, with mostly old women around. It looked to me almost literary and Elbert Hubbardish compared to the Grand Central in Shelby. The folks there stared at me somewhat suspiciously and I half thought they were going to say they didn't take pedlars; but when I flashed a new five-dollar bill at the desk I got good service. A five-dollar bill is a patent of nobility in New England.

My! how I enjoyed that creamed chicken on toast, and buckwheat cakes with syrup! After you get used to cooking all your own grub, a meal off some one else's stove is the finest kind of treat. After supper I was all prepared to sit out on the porch with my sweater on and give a rocking chair a hot box, but then I remembered that it was up to me to carry on the traditions of

Parnassus. I was there to spread the gospel of good books. I got to thinking how the Professor never shirked carrying on his campaign, and I determined that I would be worthy of the cause.

When I think back about the experience, it seems pretty crazy, but at the time I was filled with a kind of evangelistic zeal. I thought if I was going to try to sell books I might as well have some fun out of it. Most of the old ladies were squatting about in the parlour, knitting or reading or playing cards. In the smoking-room I could see two dried-up men. Mrs. Hominy, the manager of the place, was sitting at her desk behind a brass railing, going over accounts with a quill pen. I thought that the house probably hadn't had a shock since Walt Whitman wrote "Leaves of Grass." In a kind of do-or-die spirit I determined to give them a rouse.

In the dining-room I had noticed a huge dinner bell that stood behind the door. I stepped in there, and got it. Standing in the big hall I began ringing it as hard as I could shake my arm.

You might have thought it was a fire alarm. Mrs. Hominy dropped her pen in horror. The colonial dames in the parlour came to life and ran into the hall like cockroaches. In a minute I had gathered quite a respectable audience. It was up to me to do the spellbinding.

"Friends," I said (unconsciously imitating the Professor's tricks of the trade, I guess), "this bell which generally summons you to the groaning board now calls you to a literary repast. With the permission of the management, and with apologies for disturbing your tranquillity, I will deliver a few remarks on the value of good books. I see that several of you are fond of reading, so perhaps the topic will be congenial?"

They gazed at me about as warmly as a round of walnut sundaes.

"Ladies and Gentlemen," I continued, "of course you remember the story of Abe Lincoln when he said, 'if you call a leg a tail, how many tails has a dog?' 'Five,' you answer. Wrong; because, as Mr. Lincoln said, calling a leg a tail...."

I still think it was a good beginning. But that was as far as I got. Mrs. Hominy came out of her trance, hastened from the cage, and grabbed my arm. She was quite red with anger.

"Really!" she said. "Well, really!... I must ask you to continue this in some other place. We do not allow commercial travellers in this house."

And within fifteen minutes they had hitched up Peg and asked me to move on. Indeed I was so taken aback by my own zeal that I could hardly protest. In a kind of daze I found myself at the Moose Hotel, where they assured me that they catered to mercantile people. I went straight to my room and fell asleep as soon as I reached the straw mattress.

That was my first and only pubic speech.

Chapter 12

The next day was Sunday, October sixth. I well remember the date.

I woke up as chipper as any Robert W. Chambers heroine. All my doubts and depressions of the evening before had fled, and I was single-heartedly delighted with the world and everything in it. The hotel was a poor place, but it would have taken more than that to mar my composure. I had a bitterly cold bath in a real country tin tub, and then eggs and pancakes for breakfast. At the table was a drummer who sold lightning rods, and several other travelling salesmen. I'm afraid my conversation was consciously modelled along the line of what the Professor would have said if he had been there, but at any rate I got along swimmingly. The travelling men, after a moment or two of embarrassed diffidence, treated me quite as one of themselves and asked me about my "line" with interest. I described what I was doing and they all said they envied me my freedom to come and go independently of trains. We talked cheerfully for a long time, and almost without intending to, I started preaching about books. In the end they insisted on my showing them Parnassus. We all went out to the stable, where the van was quartered, and they browsed over the shelves. Before I knew it I had sold five dollars' worth, although I had decided not to do any business at all on Sunday. But I couldn't refuse to sell them the stuff as they all seemed so keen on getting something really good to read. One man kept on talking about Harold Bell Wright, but I had to admit that I hadn't heard of him. Evidently the Professor hadn't stocked any of his works. I was tickled to see that after all little Redbeard didn't know *everything* about literature.

After that I debated whether to go to church or to write letters. Finally I decided in favour of the letters. First I tackled Andrew.

I wrote:

> The Moose Hotel, Bath,
> Sunday morning.
>
> **DEAR ANDREW:**
>
> It seems absurd to think that it's only three days since I left Sabine Farm. Honestly, more has happened to me in these three days than in three years at home. I'm sorry that you and Mr. Mifflin disagreed but I quite understood your feelings. But I'm very angry that you should have tried to stop that check I gave him. It was none of your business, Andrew. I telephoned Mr. Shirley and made him send word to the bank in Woodbridge to give Mifflin the money. Mr. Mifflin did not swindle me into buying Parnassus. I did it of my own free will. If you want to know the truth, it was your fault! I bought it because I was scared *you* would if I didn't. And I didn't want to be left all alone on the farm from now till Thanksgiving while you went off on another trip. So I decided to do the thing myself. I thought I'd see how you

100

would like being left all alone to run the house. I thought it'd be pretty nice for me to get things off my mind a while and have an adventure of my own.

Now, Andrew, here are some directions for you:

1. Don't forget to feed the chickens twice a day, and collect *all* the eggs. There's a nest behind the wood pile, and some of the Wyandottes have been laying under the ice house.

2. Don't let Rosie touch grandmother's blue china, because she'll break it as sure as fate if she lays her big, thick Swedish fingers on it.

3. Don't forget your warmer underwear. The nights are getting chilly.

4. I forgot to put the cover on the sewing machine. Please do that for me or it'll get all dusty.

5. Don't let the cat run loose in the house at night: he always breaks something.

6. Send your socks and anything else that needs darning over to Mrs. McNally, she can do it for you.

7. Don't forget to feed the pigs.

8. Don't forget to mend the weathervane on the barn.

9. Don't forget to send that barrel of apples over to the cider mill or you won't have any cider to drink when Mr. Decameron comes up to see us later in the fall.

10. Just to make ten commandments, I'll add one more: You might 'phone to Mrs. Collins that the Dorcas will have to meet at some one else's house next week, because I

don't know just when I'll get back. I may be
away a fortnight more. This is my first
holiday in a long time and I'm going to
chew it before I swallow it.

The Professor (Mr. Mifflin, I mean) has
gone back to Brooklyn to work on his book.
I'm sorry you and he had to mix it up on the
high road like a couple of hooligans. He's a
nice little man and you'd like him if you got
to know him.

I'm spending Sunday in Bath: to-morrow
I'm going on toward Hastings.

I've sold five dollars' worth of books this
morning even if it is
Sunday.

Your affte sister
HELEN McGiLL.

P.S. Don't forget to clean the separator after
using it, or it'll get in a fearful state.

After writing to Andrew I thought I would send a
message to the Professor. I had already written him a
long letter in my mind, but somehow when I began
putting it on paper a sort of awkwardness came over me.
I didn't know just how to begin. I thought how much
more fun it would be if he were there himself and I
could listen to him talk. And then, while I was writing
the first few sentences, some of the drummers came
back into the room.

"Thought you'd like to see a Sunday paper," said one
of them.

I picked up the newspaper with a word of thanks and
ran an eye over the headlines. The ugly black letters
stood up before me, and my heart gave a great
contraction. I felt my fingertips turn cold.

102

DISASTROUS WRECK
ON THE SHORE LINE
EXPRESS RUNS INTO OPEN SWITCH

—

TEN LIVES LOST, AND
MORE THAN A SCORE INJURED

—

FAILURE OF BLOCK SIGNALS

The letters seemed to stand up before me as large as a Malted Milk signboard. With a shuddering apprehension I read the details. Apparently the express that left Providence at four o'clock on Saturday afternoon had crashed into an open siding near Willdon about six o'clock, and collided with a string of freight empties. The baggage car had been demolished and the smoker had turned over and gone down an embankment. There were ten men killed... my head swam. Was that the train the Professor had taken? Let me see. He left Woodbridge on a local train at three. He had said the day before that the express left Port Vigor at five.... If he had changed to the express.....

In a kind of fascinated horror my eye caught the list of   the   dead. I ran down the names. Thank God, no, Mifflin was not among   them. Then I saw the last entry:

UNIDENTIFIED MAN, MIDDLE-AGED.

What if that should be the Professor?

And I suddenly felt dizzy, and for the first time in my life I fainted.

Thank goodness, no one else was in the room. The drummers had gone outside again, and no one heard me flop off the chair. I came to in a moment, my heart whirling like a spinning top. At first I did not realize what was wrong. Then my eye fell on the newspaper again. Feverishly I re-read the account, and the names of the injured, too, which I had missed before. Nowhere was there a name I knew. But the tragic words "unidentified man" danced before my eyes. Oh! if it were the Professor....

In a wave the truth burst upon me. I loved that little man: I loved him, I loved him. He had brought something new into my life, and his brave, quaint ways had warmed my fat old heart. For the first time, in an intolerable gush of pain, I seemed to know that my life could never again be endurable without him. And now—what was I to do?

How could I learn the truth? Certainly if he *had* been on the train, and had escaped from the wreck unhurt, he would have sent a message to Sabine Farm to let me know. At any rate, that was a possibility. I rushed to the telephone to call up Andrew.

Oh! the agonizing slowness of telephone connections when urgent hurry is needed! My voice shook as I said "Redfield 158 J" to the operator. Throbbing with nervousness I waited to hear the familiar click of the receiver at the other end. I could hear the Redfield switchboard receive the call, and put in the plug to connect with our wire. In imagination I could see the telephone against the wall in the old hallway at Sabine Farm. I could see the soiled patch of plaster where Andrew rests his elbow when he talks into the 'phone, and the place where he jots numbers down in pencil and I rub them off with bread crumbs. I could see Andrew coming out of the sitting-room to answer the bell. And then the operator said carelessly, "Doesn't answer." My forehead was wet as I came out of the booth.

I hope I may never have to re-live the horrors of the next hour. In spite of my bluff and hearty ways, in times of trouble I am as reticent as a clam. I was determined to hide my agony and anxiety from the well-meaning people of the Moose Hotel. I hurried to the railway station to send a telegram to the Professor's address in Brooklyn, but found the place closed. A boy told me it would not be open until the afternoon. From a drugstore I called "information" in Willdon, and finally got connected with some undertaker to whom the Willdon operator referred me. A horrible, condoling voice (have you ever talked to an undertaker over the telephone?) answered me that no one by the name of Mifflin had been among the dead, but admitted that there was one body still unidentified. He used one ghastly word that made me shudder—unrecognizable. I rang off.

I knew then for the first time the horror of loneliness. I thought of the poor little man's notebook that I had seen. I thought of his fearless and lovable ways—of his pathetic little tweed cap, of the missing button of his jacket, of the bungling darns on his frayed sleeve. It seemed to me that heaven could mean nothing more than to roll creaking along country roads, in Parnassus, with the Professor beside me on the seat. What if I had known him only—how long was it? He had brought the splendour of an ideal into my humdrum life. And now—had I lost it forever? Andrew and the farm seemed faint and far away. I was a homely old woman, mortally lonely and helpless. In my perplexity I walked to the outskirts of the village and burst into tears.

Finally I got a grip on myself again. I am not ashamed to say that I now admitted frankly what I had been hiding from myself. I was in love—in love with a little, red-bearded bookseller who seemed to me more splendid than Sir Galahad. And I vowed that if he would have me, I would follow him to the other end of nowhere.

I walked back to the hotel. I thought I would make one more try to get Andrew on the telephone. My whole soul quivered when at last I heard the receiver click.

"Hello?" said Andrew's voice.

"Oh, Andrew," I said, "this is Helen."

"Where are you?" (His voice sounded cross.)

"Andrew, is there any—any message from Mr. Mifflin? That wreck yesterday—he might have been on that train—I've been so frightened; do you think he was—hurt?"

"Stuff and nonsense," said Andrew. "If you want to know   about Mifflin, he's in jail in Port Vigor."

And then I think Andrew must have been surprised. I began to laugh and cry simultaneously, and in my agitation   I   set   down   the   receiver.

Chapter 13

My first impulse was to hide myself in some obscure corner where I could vent my feelings without fear or favour. I composed my face as well as I could before leaving the 'phone booth; then I sidled across the lobby and slipped out of the side door. I found my way into the stable, where good old Peg was munching in her stall. The fine, homely smell of horseflesh and long-worn harness leather went right to my heart, and while Bock frisked at my knees I laid my head on Peg's neck and cried. I think that fat old mare understood me. She was as tubby and prosaic and middle-aged as I—but she loved the Professor.

Suddenly Andrew's words echoed again in my mind. I had barely heeded them before, in the great joy of my relief, but now their significance came to me. "In jail." The Professor in jail! That was the meaning of his strange disappearance at Woodbridge. That little brute of a man Shirley must have telephoned from Redfield, and when the Professor came to the Woodbridge bank to cash that check they had arrested him. That was why they had shoved me into that mahogany sitting-room. Andrew must be behind this. The besotted old fool! My face burned with anger and humiliation.

I never knew before what it means to be really infuriated. I could feel my brain tingle. The Professor in jail! The gallant, chivalrous little man, penned up with hoboes and sneak thieves suspected of being a crook...

as if I couldn't take care of myself! What did they think he was, anyway? A kidnapper?

Instantly I decided I would hurry back to Port Vigor without delay. If Andrew had had the Professor locked up, it could only be on the charge of defrauding me. Certainly it couldn't be for giving him a bloody nose on the road from Shelby. And if I appeared to deny the charge, surely they would have to let Mr. Mifflin go.

I believe I must have been talking to myself in Peg's stall—at any rate, just at this moment the stableman appeared and looked very bewildered when he saw me, with flushed face and in obvious excitement, talking to the horse. I asked him when was the next train to Port Vigor.

"Well, ma'am," he said, "they say that all the local trains is held up till the wreck at Willdon's cleared away. This being Sunday, I don't think you'll get anything from here until to-morrow morning."

I reflected. It wasn't so awfully far back to Port Vigor. A flivver from the local garage could spin me back there in a couple of hours at the most. But somehow it seemed more fitting to go to the Professor's rescue in his own Parnassus, even if it would take longer to get there. To tell the truth, while I was angry and humiliated at the thought of his being put in jail by Andrew, I couldn't help, deep down within me, being rather thankful. Suppose he had been in the wreck? The Sage of Redfield had played the part of Providence after all. And if I set out right away with Parnassus, I could get to Port Vigor—well, by Monday morning anyway.

The good people of the Moose Hotel were genuinely surprised at the hurry with which I dispatched my lunch. But I gave them no explanations. Goodness knows, my head was full of other thoughts and the apple sauce might have been asbestos. You know, a woman only falls in love once in her life, and if it waits until she's darn near forty—well, it *takes!* You see I hadn't even been vaccinated against it by girlish flirtations. I began to be a governess when I was just a kid, and a governess doesn't get many chances to be skittish. So now when it came, it hit me hard. That's when a woman finds herself—when she's in love. I don't care if she *is* old or fat or homely or prosy. She feels that little flutter under her ribs and she drops from the tree like a ripe plum. I didn't care if Roger Mifflin and I were as odd a couple as old Dr. Johnson and his wife, I only knew one thing: that when I saw that little red devil again I was going to be all his—if he'd have me. That's why the old Moose Hotel in Bath is always sacred to me. That's where I learned that life still held something fresh for me— something better than baking champlain biscuits for Andrew.

* * * * * * * * *

That Sunday was one of those mellow, golden days that we New Englanders get in October. The year really begins in March, as every farmer knows, and by the end of September or the beginning of October the season has come to its perfect, ripened climax. There are a few days when the world seems to hang still in a dreaming, sweet hush, at the very fulness of the fruit before the decline sets in. I have no words (like Andrew) to describe it, but every autumn for years I have noticed it. I remember that sometimes at the farm I used to lean over the wood pile for a moment just before supper to watch those purple October sunsets. I would hear the sharp ting of Andrew's little typewriter bell as he was working in his study. And then I would try to swallow down within me the beauty and wistfulness of it all, and run back to mash the potatoes.

Peg drew Parnassus along the backward road with a merry little rumble. I think she knew we were going back to the Professor. Bock careered mightily along the wayside. And I had much time for thinking. On the whole, I was glad; for I had much to ponder. An adventure that had started as a mere lark or whim had now become for me the very gist of life itself. I was fanciful, I guess, and as romantic as a young hen, but by the bones of George Eliot, I'm sorry for the woman that never has a chance to be fanciful. Mifflin was in jail; aye, but he might have been dead and—unrecognizable! My heart refused to be altogether sad. I was on my way to deliver him from durance vile. There seemed a kinship between the season and myself, I mused, seeing the goldenrod turning bronze and droopy along the way. Here was I, in the full fruition of womanhood, on the verge of my decline into autumn, and lo! by the grace of God, I had found my man, my master. He had touched me with his own fire and courage. I didn't care what happened to Andrew, or to Sabine Farm, or to anything else in the world. Here were my hearth and my home— Parnassus, or wherever Roger should pitch his tent. I dreamed of crossing the Brooklyn Bridge with him at dusk, watching the skyscrapers etched against a burning sky. I believed in calling things by their true names. Ink is ink, even if the bottle is marked "commercial fluid." I didn't try to blink the fact that I was in love. In fact, I gloried in it. As Parnassus rolled along the road, and the scarlet maple leaves eddied gently down in the blue October air, I made up a kind of chant which I called

> Hymn for a Middle-Aged Woman (Fat)
> Who Has Fallen into Love
> O God, I thank Thee who sent this great
> adventure my way! I am grateful to have
> come out of the barren land of spinsterhood,
> seeing the glory of a love greater than
> myself. I thank Thee for teaching me that
> mixing, and kneading, and baking are not

all that life holds for me. Even if he doesn't
love me, God, I shall always be his.

I was crooning some such babble as this to myself
when, near Woodbridge, I came upon a big, shiny motor
car stranded by the roadside. Several people, evidently
intelligent and well-to-do, sat under a tree while their
chauffeur fussed with a tire. I was so absorbed in my
own thoughts that I think I should have gone by without
paying them much heed, but suddenly I remembered the
Professor's creed—to preach the gospel of books in and
out of season. Sunday or no Sunday, I thought I could
best honour Mifflin by acting on his own principle. I
pulled up by the side of the road.

I noticed the people turn to one another in a kind of
surprise, and whisper something. There was an elderly
man with a lean, hard-worked face; a stout woman,
evidently his wife; and two young girls and a man in
golfing clothes. Somehow the face of the older man
seemed familiar. I wondered whether he were some
literary friend of Andrew's whose photo I had seen.

Bock stood by the wheel with his long, curly tongue
running in and out over his teeth. I hesitated a moment,
thinking just how to phrase my attack, when the elderly
gentleman called out:

"Where's the Professor?"

I was beginning to realize that Mifflin was indeed a
public character.

"Heavens!" I said. "Do you know him, too?"

"Well, I should think so," he said. "Didn't he come to
see me last spring about an appropriation for school
libraries, and wouldn't leave till I'd promised to do what
he wanted! He stayed the night with us and we talked
literature till four o'clock in the morning. Where is he
now? Have you taken over Parnassus?"

"Just at present," I said, "Mr. Mifflin is in the jail at Port Vigor."

The ladies gave little cries of astonishment, and the gentleman himself (I had sized him up as a school commissioner or something of that sort) seemed not less surprised.

"In jail!" he said. "What on earth for? Has he sandbagged somebody for reading Nick Carter and Bertha M. Clay? That's about the only crime he'd be likely to commit."

"He's supposed to have cozened me out of four hundred dollars," I said, "and my brother has had him locked up. But as a matter of fact he wouldn't swindle a hen out of a new-laid egg. I bought Parnassus of my own free will. I'm on my way to Port Vigor now to get him out. Then I'm going to ask him to marry me—if he will. It's not leap year, either."

He looked at me, his thin, lined face working with friendliness. He was a fine-looking man—short, gray hair brushed away from a broad, brown forehead. I noticed his rich, dark suit and the spotless collar. This was a man of breeding, evidently.

"Well, Madam," he said, "any friend of the Professor is a friend of ours." (His wife and the girls chimed in with assent.) "If you would like a lift in our car to speed you on your errand, I'm sure Bob here would be glad to drive Parnassus into Port Vigor. Our tire will soon be mended."

The young man assented heartily, but as I said before, I was bent on taking Parnassus back myself. I thought the sight of his own tabernacle would be the best balm for Mifflin's annoying experience. So I refused the offer, and explained the situation a little more fully.

"Well," he said, "then let me help in any way I can." He took a card from his pocket-book and scribbled something on it. "When you get to Port Vigor," he said,

112

"show this at the jail and I don't think you'll have any trouble. I happen to know the people there."

So after a hand-shake all round I went on again, much cheered by this friendly little incident. It wasn't till I was some way along the road that I thought of looking at the card he had given me. Then I realized why the man's face had been familiar. The card read quite simply:

RALEIGH STONE STAFFORD

The Executive Mansion,
Darlington.
It was the Governor of the State!

Chapter 14

I couldn't help chuckling, as Parnassus came over the brow of the hill, and I saw the river in the distance once more. How different all this was from my girlhood visions of romance. That has been characteristic of my life all along—it has been full of homely, workaday happenings, and often rather comic in spite of my best resolves to be highbrow and serious. All the same I was something near to tears as I thought of the tragic wreck at Willdon and the grief-laden hearts that must be mourning. I wondered whether the Governor was now returning from Willdon after ordering an inquiry.

On his card he had written: "Please release R. Mifflin at once and show this lady all courtesies." So I didn't anticipate any particular trouble. This made me all the more anxious to push on, and after crossing the ferry we halted in Woodbridge only long enough for supper. I drove past the bank where I had waited in the anteroom, and would have been glad of a chance to horsewhip that sneaking little cashier. I wondered how they had transported the Professor to Port Vigor, and thought ironically that it was only that Saturday morning when he had suggested taking the hoboes to the same jail. Still I do not doubt that his philosophic spirit had made the best of it all.

Woodbridge was as dead as any country town is on Sunday night. At the little hotel where I had supper there was no topic of conversation except the wreck. But the proprietor, when I paid my bill, happened to notice Parnassus in the yard.

"That's the bus that pedlar sold you, ain't it?" he asked with a leer.

"Yes," I said, shortly.

"Goin' back to prosecute him, I guess?" he suggested. "Say, that feller's a devil, believe *me*. When the sheriff tried to put the cuffs on him he gave him a black eye and pretty near broke his jaw. Some scrapper fer a midget!"

My own brave little fighter, I thought, and flushed with pride.

The road back to Port Vigor seemed endless. I was a little nervous, remembering the tramps in Pratt's quarry, but with Bock sitting beside me on the seat I thought it craven to be alarmed. We rumbled gently through the darkness, between aisles of inky pines where the strip of starlight ran like a ribbon overhead, then on the rolling dunes that overlook the water. There was a moon, too, but I was mortally tired and lonely and longed only to see my little Redbeard. Peg was weary, too, and plodded slowly. It must have been midnight before we saw the red and green lights of the railway signals and I knew that Port Vigor was at hand.

I decided to camp where I was. I guided Peg into a field beside the road, hitched her to a fence, and took the dog into the van with me. I was too tired to undress. I fell into the bunk and drew the blankets over me. As I did so, something dropped down behind the bunk with a sharp rap. It was a forgotten corncob pipe of the Professor's, blackened and sooty. I put it under my pillow, and fell asleep.

Monday, October seventh. If this were a novel about some charming, slender, pansy-eyed girl, how differently I would have to describe the feelings with which I woke the next morning. But these being only a few pages from the life of a fat, New England housewife, I must be candid. I woke feeling dull and sour. The day was gray and cool: faint shreds of mist sifting up from the Sound and a desolate mewing of seagulls in the air. I was unhappy, upset, and—yes— shy. Passionately I yearned to run to the Professor, to gather him into my arms, to be alone with him in Parnassus, creaking up some sunny by-road. But his words came back to me: I was nothing to him. What if he didn't love me after all?

I walked across two fields, down to the beach where little waves were slapping against the shingle. I washed my face and hands in salt water. Then I went back to Parnassus and brewed some coffee with condensed milk. I gave Peg and Bock their breakfasts. Then I hitched Peg to the van again, and felt better. As I drove into the town I had to wait at the grade crossing while a wrecking train rumbled past, on its way back from Willdon. That meant that the line was clear again. I watched the grimy men on the cars, and shuddered to think what they had been doing.

The Vigor county jail lies about a mile out of the town, an ugly, gray stone barracks with a high, spiked wall about it. I was thankful that it was still fairly early in the morning, and I drove through the streets without seeing any one I knew. Finally I reached the gate in the prison wall. Here some kind of a keeper barred my way. "Can't get in, lady," he said. "Yesterday was visitors' day. No more visitors till next month."

"I *must* get in," I said. "You've got a man in there on a false charge."

"So they all say," he retorted, calmly, and spat halfway across the road. "You wouldn't believe any of our boarders had a right to be here if you could hear their friends talk."

I showed him Governor Stafford's card. He was rather impressed by this, and retired into a sentry-box in the wall—to telephone, I suppose.

Presently he came back.

"The sheriff says he'll see you, ma'am. But you'll have to leave this here dynamite caboose behind." He unlocked a little door in the immense iron gate, and turned me over to another man inside. "Take this here lady to the sheriff," he said.

Some of Vigor county's prisoners must have learned to be pretty good gardeners, for certainly the grounds were in good condition. The grass was green and trimly mowed; there were conventional beds of flowers in very ugly shapes; in the distance I saw a gang of men in striped overalls mending a roadway. The guide led me to an attractive cottage to one side of the main building. There were two children playing outside, and I remember thinking that within the walls of a jail was surely a queer place to bring up youngsters.

But I had other things to think about. I looked up at that grim, gray building. Behind one of those little barred windows was the Professor. I should have been angry at Andrew, but somehow it all seemed a kind of dream. Then I was taken into the hallway of the sheriff's cottage and in a minute I was talking to a big, bull-necked man with a political moustache.

"You have a prisoner here called Roger Mifflin?" I said.

"My dear Madam, I don't keep a list of all our inmates in my head. If you will come to the office we will look up the records."

I showed him the Governor's card. He took it and kept looking at it as though he expected to see the message written there change or fade away. We walked across a strip of lawn to the prison building. There, in a big bare office, he ran over a card index.

"Here we are," he said. "Roger Mifflin; age, 41; face, oval; complexion, florid; hair, red but not much of it; height, 64 inches; weight, stripped, 120; birthmark...."

"Never mind," I said. "That's the man. What's he here for?"

"He's held in default of bail, pending trial. The charge is attempt to defraud one Helen McGill, spinster, age..."

"Rubbish!" I said. "I'm Helen McGill, and the man made no attempt to defraud me."

"The charge was entered and warrant applied for by your   brother, Andrew McGill, acting on your behalf."

"I never authorized Andrew to act on my behalf."

"Then do you withdraw the charge?"

"By all means," I said. "I've a great mind to enter a counter-charge against Andrew and have *him* arrested."

"This is all very irregular," said the sheriff, "but if the prisoner is known to the Governor, I suppose there is no alternative. I cannot annul the warrant without some recognizance. According to the laws of this State the next of kin must stand surety for the prisoner's good behaviour after release. There is no next of kin...."

"Surely there is!" I said. "I am the prisoner's next of kin."

"What do you mean?" he said. "In what relationship do you stand to this Roger Mifflin?"

"I intend to marry him just as soon as I can get him away from here."

He burst into a roar of laughter. "I guess there's no stopping you," he said. He pinned the Governor's card to a blue paper on the desk, and began filling in some blanks.

"Well, Miss McGill," he went on, "don't take away more than one of my prisoners or I'll lose my job. The turnkey will take you up to the cell. I'm exceedingly sorry: you can see that the mistake was none of our fault. Tell the Governor that, will you, when you see him?"

I followed the attendant up two flights of bare, stone stairs, and down a long, whitewashed corridor. It was a gruesome place; rows and rows of heavy doors with little, barred windows. I noticed that each door had a combination knob, like a safe. My knees felt awfully shaky.

But it wasn't really so heart-throbby as I had expected. The jailer stopped at the end of a long passageway. He spun the clicking dial, while I waited in a kind of horror. I think I expected to see the Professor with shaved head (they couldn't shave much off his head, poor lamb!) and striped canvas suit, and a ball and chain on his ankle.

The door swung open heavily. There was a narrow, clean little room with a low camp bed, and under the barred window a table strewn with sheets of paper. It was the Professor in his own clothes, writing busily, with his back toward me. Perhaps he thought it was only an attendant with food, or perhaps he didn't even hear the interruption. I could hear his pen running busily. I might have known you never would get any heroics out of that man! Trust him to make the best of it!

"Lemon sole and a glass of sherry, please, James," said the Professor over his shoulder, and the warder, who evidently had joked with him before, broke into a cackle of laughter.

"A lady to see yer Lordship," he said.

The Professor turned round. His face went quite white. For the first time in my experience of him he seemed to be at a loss for speech.

"Miss—Miss McGill," he stammered. "You *are* the good Samaritan. I'm doing the John Bunyan act, see? Writing in prison. I've really started my book at last.

And I find the fellows here know nothing whatever about literature. There isn't even a library in the place."

For the life of me, I couldn't utter the tenderness in my heart with that gorilla of a jailer standing behind us.

Somehow we made our way downstairs, after the Professor had gathered together the sheets of his manuscript. It had already reached formidable proportions, as he had written fifty pages in the thirty-six hours he had been in prison. In the office we had to sign some papers. The sheriff was very apologetic to Mifflin, and offered to take him back to town in his car, but I explained that Parnassus was waiting at the gate. The Professor's eyes brightened when he heard that, but I had to hurry him away from an argument about putting good books in prisons. The sheriff walked with us to the gate and there shook hands again.

Peg whickered as we came up to her, and the Professor patted her soft nose. Bock tugged at his chain in a frenzy of joy. At last we were alone.

Chapter 15

I never knew just how it happened. Instead of driving back through Port Vigor, we turned into a side road leading up over the hill and across the heath where the air came fresh and sweet from the sea. The Professor sat very silent, looking about him. There was a grove of birches on the hill, and the sunlight played upon their satin boles.

"It feels good to be out again," he said calmly. "The Sage cannot be so keen a lover of open air as his books would indicate, or he wouldn't be so ready to clap a man into quod. Perhaps I owe him another punch on the nose for that."

"Oh, Roger," I said—and I'm afraid my voice was trembly—"I'm *sorry*. I'm *sorry*."

Not very eloquent, was it? And then, somehow or other, his arm was around me.

"Helen," he said. "Will you marry me? I'm not rich, but I've saved up enough to live on. We'll always have Parnassus, and this winter we'll go and live in Brooklyn and write the book. And we'll travel around with Peg, and preach the love of books and the love of human beings. Helen—you're just what I need, God bless you. Will you come with me and make me the happiest bookseller in the world?"

Peg must have been astonished at the length of time she had for cropping the grass, undisturbed. I know that Roger and I sat careless of time. And when he told me that ever since our first afternoon together he had determined to have me, sooner or later, I was the proudest woman in New England. I told Roger about the ghastly wreck, and my agony of apprehension. I think it was the wreck that made us both feel inclined to forgive Andrew.

We had a light luncheon together there on the dunes above the Sound. By taking a short cut over the ridge we struck into the Shelby road without going down into Port Vigor again. Peg pulled us along toward Greenbriar, and we talked as we went.

Perhaps the best of it was that a cold drizzle of rain began to fall as we moved along the hill road. The Professor—as I still call him, by force of habit—curtined in the front of the van with a rubber sheet. Bock hopped up and curled himself aginst his master's leg. Roger got out his corncob pipe, and I sat close to him. In the gathering gloom we plodded along, as happy a trio—or quartet, if you include fat, cheery old Peg—as any on this planet. Summer was over, and we were no longer young, but there were great things before us. I listened to the drip of the rain, and the steady creak of Parnassus on her axles. I thought of my "anthology" of loaves of bread and vowed to bake a million more if Roger wanted me to. It was after supper time when we got to Greenbriar. Roger had suggested that we take a shorter road that would have brought us through to Redfield sooner, but I begged him to go by way of Shelby and Greenbriar, just as we had come before. I did not tell him why I wanted this. And when finally we came to a halt in front of Kirby's store at the crossroads it was raining heavily and we were ready for a rest.

"Well, sweetheart," said Roger, "shall we go and see what sort of rooms the hotel has?"

"I can think of something better than that," said I. "Let's go up to Mr. Kane and have him marry us. Then we can get back to Sabine Farm afterward, and give Andrew a surprise."

"By the bones of Hymen!" said Roger. "You're right!"

It must have been ten o'clock when we turned in at the red gate of Sabine Farm. The rain had stopped, but the wheels sloshed through mud and water at every turn. The light was burning in the sitting-room, and through the window I could see Andrew bent over his work table. We climbed out, stiff and sore from the long ride. I saw Roger's face set in a comical blend of sternness and humour.

"Well, here goes to surprise the Sage!" he whispered.

We picked our way between puddles and rapped on the door. Andrew appeared, carrying the lamp in one hand. When he saw us he grunted.

"Let me introduce my wife," said Roger.

"Well, I'll be damned," said Andrew.

But Andrew isn't quite so black as I've painted him. When he's once convinced of the error of his ways, he is almost pathetically eager to make up. I remember only one remark in the subsequent conversation, because I was so appalled by the state of everything at Sabine Farm that I immediately set about putting the house to rights. The two men, however, as soon as Parnassus was housed in the barn and the animals under cover, sat down by the stove to talk things over.

"I tell you what," said Andrew—"do whatever you like with your wife; she's too much for me. But I'd like to buy that Parnassus."

"Not on your life!" said the Professor.

Made in the USA
Columbia, SC
07 May 2021